IS STEVIE REALLY ON GOOD BEHAVIOR THIS YEAR?

Carole groaned. "April Fools' Day again! I hate it."

Stevie poured a bag of grain into the mixing bin. "Why, Carole. How could you say such a thing?"

"Easily," Carole said. "If I recall correctly, one year you replaced Mrs. Reg's reading glasses with another pair. And then there was the time you moved all the horses into different stalls. Was that the same year you put the rubber horse manure in Mrs. diAngelo's Mercedes-Benz?"

Stevie stirred the grains together thoughtfully. "I think they were all the same year," she said. "The year before was when I—"

"Stop! I can't stand it," Carole said. "Your April Fools' pranks have been nothing but trouble. You just can't get away with this stuff all the time, Stevie."

"This year I'm only going to do nice things," Stevie promised.

Carole thought that sounded like a good idea. April Fools' Day and Stevie could be a pretty dangerous combination. . . .

THE SADDLE CLUB

BRIDLE PATH

BONNIE BRYANT

A BANTAM SKYLARK BOOK®

NEW YORK • TORONTO • LONDON • SYDNEY • AUCKLAND

RL 5, 009–012

BRIDLE PATH
A Bantam Skylark Book / April 1993

Skylark Books is a registered trademark of Bantam Books,
a division of Bantam Doubleday Dell Publishing Group, Inc.
Registered in U.S. Patent and Trademark Office and elsewhere.

"The Saddle Club" is a trademark of Bonnie Bryant Hiller.
The Saddle Club design / logo, which consists of an inverted
U-shaped design, a riding crop, and a riding hat is a
trademark of Bantam Books.

ISBN 0-553-48074-X

Published simultaneously in the United States and Canada

Bantam Books are published by Bantam Books, a division of Bantam Doubleday Dell Publishing Group, Inc. Its trademark, consist-
ing of the words "Bantam Books" and the portrayal of a rooster, is
Registered in U.S. Patent and Trademark Office and in other coun-
tries. Marca Registrada. Bantam Books, 666 Fifth Avenue, New
York, New York 10103.

PRINTED IN THE UNITED STATES OF AMERICA

CWO   0 9 8 7 6 5 4 3 2 1

CAROLE HANSON MOVED a backpack from a chair to a footstool in Stevie Lake's room so she could sit down. Lisa Atwood then moved it from the footstool to the top of a pile of magazines so she could sit down. Stevie sat on top of the backpack.

"Do you think Max will let us play mounted games today at Horse Wise?" she asked. "Last week he was so determined to have us learn everything there was about the difference between what it meant when a horse's forefoot was resting, and what it meant when its hind foot was resting, that we never got to the fun part—riding."

"Those are important things to know," Carole said,

defending Max Regnery, the owner of Pine Hollow Stables, where the girls rode. "If a horse lifts his hind foot to rest it, it means he's relaxed. If he lifts his forefoot, it means it hurts."

Carole knew a lot about horses. In fact, all three girls knew a lot about horses, but Carole probably knew the most. They all loved horses so much that they had formed their own club—The Saddle Club—and whenever they could, they had meetings, even if it meant shoving aside a lot of junk in Stevie's messy room so they could talk about their favorite subject: horses.

"I thought the chance to practice leg bandaging was useful last week," Lisa said.

Lisa always wanted to do everything the very best way she could. When it came to horses, Carole was the same. Stevie tended to be a little more casual. She loved riding and always did everything she *had* to do in order to be able to ride, but she didn't go overboard on things she considered boring. She only went overboard on things she considered fun. As a result, she was often in hot water and spent a lot of time explaining things to people like the headmistress of her school and to the director of their riding stable, Max Regnery.

Max was the owner of Pine Hollow, the stable

where the girls rode, took lessons, belonged to a Pony Club called Horse Wise, and, in Carole's case, boarded her horse. She was the only one of the three who actually owned her own horse. He was a bay gelding named Starlight. Stevie usually rode a Thoroughbred bay gelding named Topside, who had belonged to a championship show rider named Dorothy DeSoto before an accident ended Dorothy's riding career. The horse Lisa rode most these days was an Arabian named Barq.

"Well, I know we have to know things about lameness and bandaging," Stevie acknowledged, "but I'd still rather ride. I bought a whole book about horseback games, too. It's full of ideas—if I can just find it."

Stevie stood up from the magazine/backpack pile and began rummaging through another pile of books and magazines trying to locate the book of games.

She didn't find that right away, but she did find the research cards for a history paper that she'd handed in (without research cards) two months earlier. She also found her "favorite" pair of socks, though from the dust they had accumulated living underneath Stevie's radiator, it wasn't clear to Lisa and Carole what made them so special.

Neither Lisa nor Carole was as tidy as their parents

might wish, so they were reluctant to criticize their friend. But Lisa just couldn't hold it in anymore. "How do you get away with this?" she said, looking around.

"Yeah, and how do you find things to wear? I mean, what about clean clothes?" Carole asked.

"Clean clothes are over there," Stevie said, pointing to a muddled stack of unfolded items that might have been clean—or might not have been.

Lisa and Carole laughed. There really wasn't much choice. Stevie was simply incorrigible, and although being something of a slob wasn't what they loved about her, it was part of the Stevie who was their best friend, and they weren't going to change it.

There was a knock at Stevie's door, and then it opened a crack. The three girls looked over. A familiar arm reached in. It was Stevie's mother's arm, and there was a piece of paper in her hand.

"Come in," Stevie said.

"I can't," said her mother. "(A) the door won't open any farther because of a pile of something; and (B) I can't stand to look. However, all that will change shortly."

"It will?"

"Yes," said the disembodied maternal voice from the other side. "It will all change before you go to

4

Horse Wise. Because the room must be cleaned up by then."

"I don't think I have time," Stevie said, glancing around at the mess.

"No time, no Horse Wise," said her mother. "The item in my hand is a calendar. You'll note a big X marked on every Saturday. That X means that your room *must* be clean and tidy before you go to Horse Wise. Or you don't go to Horse Wise. Period."

Mrs. Lake's fingers released the calendar, and then she withdrew her hand, closing the door after her. The paper fluttered down toward the floor of Stevie's room. It came to rest on some rolled-up artwork that Stevie had brought home before Christmas vacation. Four months ago.

Stevie paled. "She means it," she said plaintively. "There's no way I can do it alone and make it to Horse Wise. You'll just have to go without me. Explain to Max. Take notes, okay? I should be able to get it all done by Monday or Tuesday, working by myself . . . if I don't stop for meals or to sleep. . . ."

"Enough, enough," Lisa said. "We'll help. Since Horse Wise is involved, it's going to be a Saddle Club project. This time."

Carole agreed. The Saddle Club had only two rules.

The first was that members had to be horse crazy, and the second was that they had to be willing to help one another out. Stevie's room definitely fell into the second category.

"We'll help you this time," Carole said pointedly, "but from now on you should try to keep it clean by doing just a little bit of work every day." Carole knew wishful thinking even when she was uttering it, but she thought she should try. She stood up and began picking at the nearest pile. She declared it to be a laundry pile and found that there was a lot to add to it. Lisa went to work on the papers. Stevie addressed the issue of clean clothes. She was surprised to find out she had so much drawer space.

The girls worked efficiently, even if it wasn't exactly what they wanted to be doing. They were a good team. They often worked together, especially at Pine Hollow, where riders were required to do chores. It was one of the ways that Max Regnery kept the costs down. Everybody pitched in.

They chatted as they worked, tossing laundry to Carole, papers to Lisa, and clean clothes to Stevie.

"You know, I'm not going to make my kids keep their rooms clean when I get married," said Stevie.

"No, you shouldn't," said Lisa. "The thing you're

going to have to do is get them to keep *your* room clean!"

"If you can find anybody who wants to marry somebody who keeps her room so messy," said Carole.

"Maybe I'll marry somebody rich enough so that we can have a maid," Stevie suggested.

"Two maids," Lisa said, looking at Carole. "And speaking of getting married and being able to afford two maids, I read in a magazine that Skye Ransom is getting married in his next movie."

Skye was a young actor whom the girls had met by accident when they were in New York. In fact, the accident had been Skye's when he fell off a horse and The Saddle Club helped him, and then made friends with him. They'd seen him again when he came to Virginia to make a movie. Lisa had even had a small part in it. The girls didn't hear from Skye often, but he was such a popular actor that they could follow his career in magazines.

"And that's just a make-believe wedding," said Stevie. "There's a real one coming up, too."

"Right, Dorothy DeSoto is getting married in just a couple of weeks. Isn't it cool that both of them are getting married at the same time?" Lisa mused dreamily, remembering that when the girls were in New

York, they'd stayed with Dorothy. They'd come to see her in the American Horse Show and had ended up seeing her in the hospital after she cracked a bone in her back, ending her show-riding career.

Stevie picked up a sweater and looked at it curiously.

"It's mine," Carole said, fetching it from Stevie's hand. "I think I lent it to you last year."

The work in Stevie's room continued then, but so did the talk about weddings.

"Isn't it romantic that Dorothy's marrying a member of the British Equestrian Team?" Carole asked. "It's sort of like a wedding that joins royal families."

Dorothy's fiancé was named Nigel Hawthorne. The girls had been following his career in equestrian magazines as avidly as they followed Skye's in teen magazines. Both Nigel and Skye were doing very well. As a member of the British Team, Nigel could compete in every important international show in the world. Dorothy would travel with him sometimes. At other times, she would remain at her stable on New York's Long Island, training show horses. Although she couldn't compete anymore, she could still train, and she did. Sometimes she trained horses she owned and that Nigel might ride. Other times owners hired her to train their horses. The life that Dorothy and her husband would live sounded just about perfect to the Saddle Club girls.

"Even their wedding is going to be horsey," said Stevie. "They're getting married at Dorothy's stable."

"On horseback?" Carole asked.

"I don't think so," said Stevie.

"But wouldn't that be perfect?" Carole asked.

Stevie cocked her head. She'd never thought about something like that, but once Stevie got to thinking about something, she often thought very fast.

"Sure, the flower girls could be on ponies," she began.

Lisa liked the idea, too. "The bride and groom could wear matching riding outfits."

"White, of course," said Carole.

"And the bride's bouquet could be made with blue ribbons," Stevie added.

"Maybe the bride and groom would be in a horse-drawn carriage," Carole suggested.

"No, but that's how they'd leave for their honeymoon," Stevie said. She sighed because it sounded so romantic.

"But the reception would have to take place in a paddock," Lisa commented.

"Unless it rained, in which case it could be in the indoor ring," Stevie said.

9

"And the food?" Carole asked.

There was a burst of laughter then from the hall outside Stevie's room. Stevie yanked on the door and found her twin brother Alex convulsed in giggles. Chad, her older brother, was in no better condition. Her younger brother, Michael, was able to report on what Alex and Chad had found so funny.

"Chad said you should eat hay at the reception," Michael said earnestly. "Alex thought the bride's bouquet should be made of manure. And I said that—"

Stevie didn't give him a chance to finish. She pounced, shrieking loudly as she landed amid her brothers. It was hard for Lisa and Carole to make out who was winning, but it seemed clear that Stevie was getting in some licks.

She didn't have time to get many in, though, because Mrs. Lake arrived.

"What's going on here?" she demanded.

"They were snooping outside my door!" Stevie said. "They were listening in and making fun."

Mrs. Lake looked at the boys. Annoyed as she was about the condition of Stevie's room, privacy was important, and in their house a closed door required respect. The boys had been breaking a household rule.

"Mom, she was talking about getting married on horseback!" Alex said in defense.

"And having flower girls on ponies!" Michael added. This brought another wave of laughter from the three boys. Mrs. Lake sighed. She looked into Stevie's room. It looked better. Not good, but better. And good enough to allow her to stop the fight that would no doubt continue the minute she left the scene. She glanced at her watch.

"Isn't it time for your Pony Club meeting?" she asked.

"Got to run!" Stevie said. She, Lisa, and Carole were out of the house in five minutes flat.

2

THE ENTIRE PONY Club was mounted on horseback shortly after the Horse Wise meeting began. This was Stevie's kind of meeting. Studying horse poses was important—even Stevie knew that. But riding was *fun*. Everybody knew that. Not only were they on horseback, but they were playing games. Max wanted to see if he could make a relay team from Horse Wise that could compete outside their own district. The Saddle Club girls decided immediately who the first three members should be, and they appreciated every opportunity to demonstrate their abilities.

They ran a tennis-racket relay race. For that one, each rider in turn had to carry a tennis racket with a ball balanced on it through a course of poles, weaving through them. They weren't allowed to touch the ball, except when it fell off the racket. That happened a lot, especially to the other riders. Stevie, Lisa, and Carole did pretty well, and their team won the race easily.

They didn't do quite so well with the Supermarket Sweep. Each rider was supposed to race around the ring, stopping at six different piles where there were stacks of shopping items that they had to put in a bag and carry to the next post. They started out pretty well, but then Lisa broke a box of eggs and that put them in third place—out of four. Carole had trouble with the roll of paper towels. When she dropped it, the roll unrolled and it took her a long time to dismount, roll it up, and get back into Starlight's saddle. By the time it was Stevie's turn, the team was a distant fourth. She decided to compensate for her disappointment by eating the cookies instead of putting them into a shopping bag. Normally Carole's seriousness and Lisa's competitiveness would have made them annoyed with Stevie, but by that time, they were so far behind in that race that they thought Stevie had a pretty good idea. They shared.

Once the other riders finished their races, they ate their cookies, too. Max, of course, had known this would happen. He provided plastic glasses and milk. It seemed to Stevie, Carole, and Lisa that no matter how hard they tried to outfox Max, he was always a step ahead of them.

"Now, while you're all quiet—and the only way I can be sure of that is to see to it that your mouths are otherwise occupied—I'm going to tell you some good news. We're going to have a visitor next week. Dorothy DeSoto will be here. She's bringing a friend—a *special* friend—"

The Saddle Club exchanged glances. This did sound like good news.

"A gentleman who is a member of the British Equestrian Team, Mr. Nigel Hawthorne. Mr. Hawthorne is here because his team is competing in the Washington Horse Show."

"Here?" asked Meg Durham, one of the Horse Wise members.

"Well, near here," Max said. Pine Hollow was in Willow Creek, Virginia, about twenty miles from Washington, D.C.

Everybody knew about the Washington Horse Show. It was a major event on the horse-show calendar, drawing the best riders from all over the United States, as well as international competitors. In certain events, national equestrian teams, usually the same riders who competed in the Olympics, participated.

"But aren't they about to get married?" Lisa blurted out, recalling the conversation the girls had while cleaning Stevie's room. "I mean, shouldn't there be parties and dress fittings—stuff like that?"

Max smiled. "Yes, they are about to get married, but business has to come before pleasure. This is going to be Nigel's last show before the wedding. His team is going on to Italy for a show in Milan after this. He and Dorothy will return to her stable on Long Island for their wedding the following weekend."

"You mean Nigel won't go to Italy?" Stevie asked. "What's the team going to do without him?"

"They'll manage," Max said. "All of these teams have a couple of alternate riders so that if one member has to be someplace or if a rider's horse is lamed and can't compete, they'll still have a full team. Nigel has somebody to stand in for him while he and Dorothy get married and have a honeymoon. Then it'll be back to business as usual. Anyway, Dorothy will be here for our meeting next week. Nigel may have to be at the show or he may be here. I've asked Dorothy to talk with you all about training championship show horses. Since we're all working together on training our colt, Samson, I'm sure we'll get a lot of useful information from her. Now, that's enough of this talking"—he said the last word as if it were something bad —"it's time to get to work and untack your horses. Each rider must groom his or her horse, and we'll have an inspection in exactly one half hour. Will you be ready?"

"Aye, aye, sir," Carole said, saluting him sharply. Her father was a colonel in the Marine Corps, and she knew how to give a proper salute. Max clicked his heels together in acknowledgment and dismissed the riders to their chores.

Carole dismounted and led Starlight to his stall. She loved to ride every bit as much as Stevie did, but she also loved all the work that went with being a horse owner. Grooming was almost as much fun as riding. She liked how shiny and wonderful Starlight looked when she did the job right. Even more, she liked how much the horse enjoyed the attention he got as she worked on him. He seemed to know when he looked good and loved to show off his gleaming coat.

First, she removed his tack and brushed it clean before she returned it to the tack room. Then she got out her grooming bucket and got to work cleaning him up.

"Don't forget to clean his hooves," Max said, looking over the door to the stall. Carole was surprised he was there. She was even more surprised that he was giving her such a basic instruction. Everybody knew that a grooming should start with picking the horse's hooves.

"No problem, Max," Carole said. She took the hoof pick out of the bucket and began the job. Max watched.

"Are you checking to see if I know how to do this or watching to see if you can pick up some pointers?" Carole asked.

"Neither, really," Max said, smiling at her attitude. "I'm just thinking. This seemed as good a place as any to do it."

"What are you thinking about?" Carole asked.

"Dorothy," he said.

"Me, too," said Carole. "I can't wait until she gets here. Nigel, too." She paused for a second. "Nope, I mean Nigel *especially*. I always like it when Dorothy's here. She's wonderful. But it's just the neatest thing that Nigel—should I call him Mr. Hawthorne?"

"Don't bother. He'll tell you to call him Nigel," Max said. Carole liked that, both about Max and about Nigel.

"Anyway, it's neat that he's this championship international competitor for England. He must be just about the *best*."

"Just about," Max agreed. "But there's something else, too. Dorothy has a stallion she wants me to buy."

This was really news.

"She's been training him for another stable, and he had an accident that will keep him out of the ring for a very long time. It's too long as far as the owners are concerned. Dorothy tells me his bloodlines are excellent, and she should know because she owns his full brother and has used him for breeding."

Carole didn't have to ask what Max meant by that. It meant that there were a lot of champions in the horse's family, and it also meant that it was likely he could sire champions, even if he never could be one himself.

Carole could hardly contain her excitement. "Are you thinking about doing more breeding here?" she asked. If a stable had a championship stallion, people who had mares would bring them to be mated with the stallion. That often meant that the mares would come to the stable to have their foals so they could be mated with the stallion soon after the birth of the foal. All of this sounded wonderful to Carole.

"Maybe," Max said. "I'm not really set up here to

be a major breeding farm, but I might do it somewhat as a sideline. What would you think about it?"

Carole didn't have to think about her answer to that question. "It would be the most wonderful thing in the whole wide world! Imagine—foals being born here all the time. It's wonderful!"

Carole and her friends had been present at the birth of Samson, the colt they were now beginning to train. It had been a little scary for them, but it had also been exciting and beautiful. Carole didn't think there was anything more exciting in the world than watching a foal take its first few steps and its first taste of mare's milk.

"Look," she said. "There are two stalls over there that we rarely use, and we can knock down one wall to make a single big stall that we can use as a second foaling box. I think the stallion will need a paddock of his own, and it shouldn't be far from the stable because stallions tend to be moody and unpredictable, so it would probably be best to have it open directly from his stall. I think the best candidate for that would be the stall on the other side, across from the tack room. It has a big window. It shouldn't be hard to turn that window into a door, and that's right by the large paddock. The stallion can make do with half that paddock, can't he? Max?"

Carole stopped because she noticed that Max was laughing. "What's so funny?" she asked.

"You," he said. "I ask you a simple question, like what do you think of the idea, and the next thing I know, you're moving walls and shifting paddocks around!"

"You don't like my ideas?" Carole asked. Her feelings were a little bit hurt.

"Oh, no, it's not that," Max said. "What's really funny is that everything you said was something I've already decided is the right way to handle this. Only it took me about a week of thinking to come up with it!"

Carole's feelings weren't hurt anymore. She was very pleased, indeed. She was even embarrassed now because she thought she might have hurt Max's feelings a little bit by being so very clever. She didn't have a chance to say anything, though, because their conversation was interrupted by the arrival of one of the stable's adult riders, Judge Gavin.

"I say there, Regnery," he said rather unpleasantly. "Have you got a decent horse for me today?"

Carole cringed on Max's behalf. *All* of Max's horses were "decent," and most of them were a lot more than that. Experience had shown Carole and her friends that it was important to match horses and riders carefully. Carole had taken on the job at the stable once while Max was away and discovered that she was pretty good at it. Max turned to her for advice now.

"Carole, what do you think?" he asked. "Judge Gavin has a lot of experience. He's a good rider and enjoys a spirited horse—"

"Comanche?" Carole suggested.

The judge grunted and then scowled. "I tried that one last week," he said. The look on his face told Carole that it had not been a successful attempt. Comanche was a spirited horse, but he wasn't difficult for a good rider. Apparently Max was hinting to Carole that Judge Gavin wasn't quite as good a rider as Judge Gavin liked to think he was. He needed a horse he *thought* was spirited. This was going to require some tact.

"Do you think he could handle Delilah?" Carole asked.

"Hmmmm," Max said. Delilah was a mare—the mother of Samson. She was a fine horse and very responsive. She was not spirited the way Comanche was. She was also quite beautiful, being a palomino, with a silvery mane. A lot of riders were awed by her beauty. "Delilah," Max said, as if he were mulling the idea some more. "Yes, I think so. A rider with the judge's experience . . . definitely, Delilah."

21

"Is she going to be too much for me?" the man asked, suddenly concerned. Max turned to Carole.

"Oh, no, Your Honor," she said. "I know your reputation. And I've watched you ride. You're tough. Delilah will recognize that right away. She's a good horse, though. I don't think she'll give you much trouble. And she hasn't been ridden yet today. Max wouldn't put any of the Pony Club children on her, so she's fresh. I think you'll be able to control her just fine."

Carole didn't look at Max. She knew that if she did, the two of them would burst out laughing.

"All right. I'll try her," the judge agreed. "Can you have her saddled up for me?"

"Certainly," Max said. "I'll get right on it. Get yourself a hat from the wall in the locker area, and we'll have you mounted up and riding in no time."

Judge Gavin followed Max away from Starlight's stall. Carole was pleased with herself until she realized that sending the judge to the hat collection might backfire. All the spare hats were hung on nails on one wall. Stevie sometimes thought it was a fun idea to arrange them to spell things, and he might not share Stevie's sense of humor. However, there was no outraged "harrumph" from the locker area, so Carole assumed that Stevie hadn't been mischievous or else the judge hadn't noticed. She sighed with relief. Judge Gavin was an important man in town and an important customer to Max. It wouldn't help Max to offend him.

Carole picked up her grooming tools and began working on Starlight's coat in earnest. She'd finished about half the job when there was a knock at the stall door. Carole looked up.

"Saddle Club meeting at TD's in half an hour?" Stevie asked.

"Sure," Carole agreed. It seemed that there were a lot of things to talk about with her friends, especially the stallion Max might buy. Lisa and Stevie were going to love this news as much as she did.

Carole applied herself to Starlight's grooming so she wouldn't keep her friends waiting. When he was shiny as could be, when his water bucket was filled and he had a fresh tick of hay, when his stall had been mucked and there was clean straw for him to stand in, then she was ready to leave. She met Lisa and Stevie in the locker area. They each changed into street clothes. They would have been perfectly happy to wear riding clothes that carried the wonderful rich smell of horses all the time. They had found that not everybody shared their love of that scent, and so they usually changed before they left Pine Hollow, especially if they were going to TD's—an ice-cream shop at the nearby shopping center.

The three girls were about to walk out the door when Mrs. Reg appeared and stood in their way. Mrs. Reg was Max's mother and served as the stable manager. She was a good friend and an occasional surrogate mother to the riders, but she was also a stickler for completed chores.

"Ahem," she said, looking straight at Stevie. "I just took a look at Topside's tack, and it seems to me that it is now more suitable to plant radishes than to put on a horse's back!"

"I just cleaned it—" Stevie began a protest.

"Well, it just got dirty, then," Mrs. Reg said. "It must be cleaned before you leave today."

Carole and Lisa looked at one another and shrugged. "Let's get to it," Carole said.

The girls returned to the tack room, where they found that Topside's tack certainly did need a soaping. It would only take a short time with three sets of hands to do the job. Stevie was pretty sure her friends wouldn't mind helping her today. Again.

3

"I DON'T THINK dusting is going to do the job," Carole said, looking at Topside's tack. "This stuff looks as if it got dragged through mud."

"It did," said Stevie. "Remember how it rained yesterday and then we went out on the trail ride? I removed Topside's tack to groom him outside because it was so nice by then, but I didn't balance the saddle right on the fence—"

Stevie didn't have to finish the story. Both Lisa and Carole remembered then that the saddle had tipped into the mud, dragging all the rest of the tack with it. They were surprised that Stevie hadn't cleaned the tack right away. It might have been easier then. But

25

that would have meant that they would have been late getting to Stevie's house for their sleepover. Stevie's motto seemed to be "Never do today what you can put off until tomorrow—especially if you can get two good friends to do it with/for you!"

Carole picked up a brush and attacked the caked-on mud on the saddle. Stevie began working on the bridle. Lisa worked on the metal parts of the tack with another brush and then soap and water.

"Guess what," Carole said, working on a particularly stubborn mud glob with her thumbnail.

"What?" Stevie asked.

"The other reason Dorothy is coming is because she's bringing a stallion for Max."

"Max doesn't need a stallion," said Lisa. "They're difficult to ride. He'd never let one of us kids ride it, and the adult riders like tame horses, too. A stallion would be crazy for riding."

Stevie saw the other side of the story right away. "You're kidding! How wonderful!"

"*I'm* not going to ride him," said Lisa. "No way!"

"He's not for riding," Stevie told her.

"What else, then?" She seemed genuinely confused.

"Breeding," explained Carole. "Max is really considering breeding on a regular basis. This horse has good bloodlines, and there are a lot of people who would like to have their foals sired by a champion. That way, the foals are more likely to be champions themselves."

"You mean we're going to have a lot of baby horses around here?" Lisa asked. Her eyes lit up.

"Sometimes," said Carole. "Breeding horses can really be a big business. If this stallion is good enough, Max can probably make a lot of money with him."

"Then why doesn't Dorothy want to keep him?" asked Lisa.

"Dorothy owns his full brother and uses him for breeding. She doesn't need another horse with identical bloodlines," Carole explained. "She was training this one, but he had an accident and isn't suitable for showing now. He's perfect for breeding, however."

"Another wedding!" Stevie mused.

"Huh?" said Carole.

"Well, it seems that everywhere I look these days, somebody's getting married. First Dorothy and Nigel, then Skye on television, and now a mare will marry this stallion."

Carole took a deep breath and got ready to explain to Stevie that horses didn't really *marry*. The sires, as father horses were called, took no part in raising the young, except for in the wild, where young horses were part of a herd of mares and foals that was led by the sole stallion in the group. On a breeding farm, mares were separated from the stallions except when they were actually being bred, and the foals that were produced would likely never even see their sires. This was not like a traditional family of humans.

"Oh, I know all that stuff," Stevie said before Carole even began. "But it's always seemed to me that there should be a little more romance to it. Of course, we don't even know who this stallion would marry, do we?"

"Sure, what good is a groom without a bride?" Lisa said. "How about Prancer?"

"I don't think so. Remember that foot?" Stevie said.

Prancer was a Thoroughbred mare that Max and the stable's vet, Judy Barker, owned together. She had been bred and trained as a racer, but a fracture in her foot had ended that. She was now being retrained as a stable and show horse. However, there was a history of weak feet in her family, and the fracture she'd suffered confirmed that. It wasn't wise to use her for breeding, because it would mean that her foals would have a good chance of acquiring the same fault.

"Okay, so if Prancer's out, then who?"

"*If* Max wants to breed one of Pine Hollow's mares at all," said Carole.

"Of course he will," Stevie said, dismissing Carole's

caution. "Or maybe just a horse that boards here. How about Garnet?" Garnet was an Arabian mare owned by a young rider, Veronica diAngelo—the one young rider the Saddle Club girls really couldn't stand because she was such a snob.

"I hope not," said Lisa. "I wouldn't want anything that nice or that exciting to happen to Veronica."

Stevie laughed because she agreed.

"I don't think so," said Carole. "If Garnet was carrying a foal, Veronica wouldn't be able to ride her for a long time. I can't see her giving up the opportunity to ride a horse as nice-looking as Garnet. And besides, all her riding clothes have been designed to coordinate with the color of Garnet's coat."

Lisa chuckled, not because Carole had said a funny thing, but because what she had said was true. Veronica was more concerned with the look of her horse than with how well she could ride it. She definitely had her priorities upside down when it came to horses, and everything else.

"Delilah!" Carole said.

Both Lisa and Stevie looked up at her.

"Definitely Delilah. Remember, she's already foaled successfully, and that's an important thing to know about a mare. It's a while since Samson was born, and he doesn't need her anymore, although, of course, a

29

mare can foal every year, no problem. Anyway, that's got to be the mare that Max would choose first."

It made sense. And one of the nicest things about it was that since Delilah belonged to the stable, she would definitely have her foal here, and the girls could be helpful, as they had been when Samson was born.

"What are you three doing here?" That was Max. "Aren't you supposed to be shoveling down your sundaes by now?"

The girls were a little surprised to learn that he knew about their traditional stop at TD's. When they stopped to think about it, though, it wasn't so surprising. Max always seemed to know everything.

"Ah, the tack," he said, confirming their suspicions. "I did notice that it needed work. A lot of it."

"It's getting it," Stevie assured him. "With a little help from my friends."

Max nodded. "Well, your friend Carole has been helpful to me today, too, so I'm glad to get a chance to thank her."

"Me?"

"Yes, you. Judge Gavin was crazy about Delilah. He's a fussy man, and I haven't been able to please him at all. You managed nicely. He says he wants to ride her again, and he kept telling me what a bright and talented young woman you are. You really impressed him in a way I haven't. I don't usually think it's a good idea to coddle my riders, but Judge Gavin is an important man in town, and I was pleased when he said he wanted to ride here. He'll probably bring me other new riders. That's good for all of us, so, thanks, Carole. Thanks very much."

"You're welcome, Max. I think I was just lucky, though."

"'Tactful' is probably the word. The man's convinced that it's his riding skill that's tamed that spirited palomino."

Lisa and Stevie thought it was pretty funny when they heard the details, but they were glad that Carole had done something good for Max.

"Listen," he said. "One of the events that Nigel is going to be competing in is called the Gambler's Choice. It's really exciting. Mom and I are planning to go with Dorothy, although there's so much work to be done around here that I'm not sure we'll be able to take the time off. Anyway, if I could get some extra tickets, would you three like to come along?"

Would they! The looks on their faces answered Max's question.

"Well, I'm not sure," he said. "There is a lot to be done. I know I'd need some help from you all—I mean like major chores, not just the routine stuff."

"We'll help," Carole said.

"Promise," Stevie added.

"Whatever it is," promised Lisa.

"And, of course, there are Pony Club jobs that need to be up-to-date."

"My notebook is almost up-to-date," Lisa said.

"Mine is," said Carole.

"Mine *will* be," said Stevie.

"And I'm not actually certain that I'll have time to call about the tickets," said Max. "I do have to sort and catalog all the specialized riding habits in the attic. Mom has told me it *has* to be done this week. . . ."

"We can do it," Lisa said. "I'm good at cataloging stuff."

"And I'm good at organizing closets and storage places," Carole said.

"And I'm good with messy rooms," Stevie said. Everybody looked at her and laughed. Even Stevie.

"Whatever it is, we'll do it," Carole said. "Promise."

"I'll try, then," Max said. "I know you girls would enjoy going to the show. The Gambler's Choice is on Friday. That's the thirty-first. Mother has a complete list of chores."

"Just give it to us," Carole said. "We'll see to it that it gets done."

"Sounds like a good deal to me," said Max. "And as I said, I'll see about tickets. If I have time. I've got to get going now. And you're about done with Topside's tack, aren't you?"

"Almost," Carole said, surveying the now shiny-clean leather in front of them.

"You know, one of the problems with one really clean saddle is that it makes all the other ones around it look dirty. Well, see you!" With that, he left.

Stevie hoisted Topside's saddle onto its rack and hung the clean bridle above it. She stood back and looked at the row of saddles. Max was right. The other five in the same row looked grungy compared to Topside's.

"Well, shall we?" she asked. Her friends shrugged in submission.

"Why not?" Carole asked.

"It only makes sense," agreed Lisa. "Remember, every little chore that we do will make it easier for Max to get us tickets for the horse show. Toss me a sponge."

They began their work in earnest.

33

4

Lisa clicked her mouse a few times, frowned, and then shook her head. That wasn't right at all, and it was getting worse. She was trying to make a chart that would list all the jobs they needed to finish by Friday, what day they should be done, and who should do them. The problem wasn't with the list, though. Clicking the computer's mouse had made a jumble of everything, and now she had to figure out how to unjumble it.

She moved the cursor to the top of the page and typed in a new first entry. It read:

Make this computer do what I want it to. Saturday. Lisa.

Well, at least that was being organized, and being organized was Lisa's strongest characteristic.

When Lisa finally finished the chart, she ran three copies on her printer and put two in envelopes for Stevie and Carole. The third she taped onto the mirror above the dresser in her room. That way she could look at it every morning and every night. Now everything was clear as could be. And what was clearest of all was that there was a *lot* of work to be done. She taped a string attached to a pencil next to the list. That way she could check off everything as it got done. She hoped she'd be able to check it all off by Friday. She sighed.

AT THE SAME time, Stevie was thinking about all the work that had to be done that week, too. Only in Stevie's mind, the major task was putting the days behind her so she could get to Friday night and go to the horse show.

She'd been to national-level horse shows before. She and her friends had watched Dorothy DeSoto compete in New York. But this was going to be even better. This time Dorothy would be sitting with them, and the man Dorothy was going to marry would be competing in one of the most exciting events there was. This wasn't just going to be wonderful, it was also going to be romantic!

There was a rustle under Stevie's bed. She rolled over onto her stomach and hung her top half over the edge of the bed. She lifted up the flounce. It took a second for her eyes to adjust to the dark and then a full minute for them to adjust to the sea of dust bunnies. Then the light caught something—two things, in fact. It was her cat, Madonna, furiously attacking something that looked like a gray ball. First, Madonna held it in her front paws and scratched at it with her hind paws. Then, when it rolled out of her grasp, she batted at it. A very dusty, very dirty sock came skittering out from under the bed. That was followed by a blue one, no cleaner than the gray one that had probably once been white. Stevie reached out for both of them and batted them back under the bed. Madonna slithered out from under the flounce then, cast an irritated glance at Stevie, and walked out of the room.

The appearance of the two socks made Stevie think about clothes in general, and since she'd also been thinking about the horse show, she began to think about what clothes she would wear to the horse show. She wouldn't wear riding clothes, of course. That was like somebody wearing a baseball uniform to watch a baseball game. Those people always made her laugh.

Stevie did, however, want to wear something a little horsey. She dismissed the idea of jeans and boots, because they seemed too casual to wear to a fancy show like this one. She considered her gray skirt and the white shirt with a white tie that she wore when she was in a show herself. No, that was too close to the baseball-uniform idea. She had a shirt with horses printed on it. That might go with her blue slacks.

She stood up and went to her closet so she could consider all the possibilities. Within a very few minutes, Stevie had almost everything she owned (except the awful dress her mother had bought for her to wear to her cousin's wedding) on the bed, and began pulling blouses and sweaters out of her drawers. Nothing seemed right. But then, there were dirty clothes to consider. Maybe she'd get some inspiration from that, and anything that was dirty now could be washed by Friday night. She pulled her laundry bag out of her closet and emptied it onto the floor. The blue turtleneck might go nicely with the blue-and-white sweater, and then her blue slacks would be nicer with it than jeans, though the top looked better with jeans. But if she wore the slacks, then she shouldn't wear boots.

She returned to her closet. She was pretty sure she had a pair of flats that would look good with the slacks. They weren't in plain sight. Maybe they were underneath the model of the planets. That came out. There were six shoes there—two pairs and two odds, both left, but no sign of the flats. Then she remembered that she'd lent the flats to someone, and she couldn't remember who it was. She looked at the shoes. One of the left odds would do. If only she could find the right one. She removed the stack of papers she'd stuck into the far corner of the closet and tossed them onto the floor by her bedside table. There it was. The right shoe that matched the left that would go with the slacks that matched the turtleneck and sweater. She had a complete outfit now. She imagined herself in it. It might be too casual for the horse show.

Stevie lay back down on her bed to consider the matter. She was actually lying on a stack of sweaters. That was more comfortable than the skirts next to her, and if she didn't move, she wouldn't wrinkle the blouses on her other side. She gazed blankly at the wall and thought about what she would really wear on Friday. Something on the wall caught her attention. It was the calendar her mother had made with all the Saturdays marked with an X, meaning her room would have to be clean by then.

No problem, she thought, looking around at the

disaster area she'd created in a matter of minutes. She had six days to put it all back. That was 144 hours. Plenty of time.

Then she looked at the calendar again. Next Friday was the thirty-first of March. That meant that next Saturday was April Fools' Day. That was usually Stevie's favorite day because it gave her a perfect excuse to play tricks, which she liked to do every day of the year but didn't always have an excuse for. On April Fools' Day, she had an excuse. It didn't take much work to figure out who she wanted to play jokes on: her brothers. Those three rats who had such fun listening at her door and teasing her and her friends; those pests who answered her phone calls, and when it was her boyfriend, Phil, were likely to say things like, "Stevie! It's for you! It's a boy! Come quick and talk to him before he hangs up like the other ones did!" Thank goodness Phil had three sisters and understood what life was really like!

Yes, her brothers, Stevie decided. She scooched along her bed until her head was comfortably on her pillow. That knocked a couple of skirts onto the floor, but that was better than lying on them, wasn't it?

"WE'RE GOING TO have a stallion, Dad. Isn't that wonderful?" Carole almost sighed with happiness as she told her father Max's great news. "I mean, I know 'we' isn't exactly the right word, but I'll be there to help with the foaling, and it'll be almost as good as if it were my stallion, my mare, and my foal, right?"

Carole's father smiled warmly at his daughter. "Sure thing, honey," he said. "And it'll be a lot cheaper for me to have Max own all those horses than for me to own them!"

"It's not funny, Dad," said Carole. "One day I'm going to own a stallion and breed horses."

"I thought you wanted to be a trainer like Dorothy DeSoto," he reminded her.

"I do. I also want to breed. And I want to ride. And I want to be a vet. And I think I should be a farrier, too. Horse shoes are very important to a horse's performance, you know."

"Don't forget stable hand," her father suggested. "I mean, just in case you need another career!"

"I promise you that one day I will choose," Carole said. "Until then, I get to dream about doing them all, don't I?"

"Sure thing," her father said. "Enjoy it, too. Dreams are free. Now tell me again about this horse show."

Carole was glad to oblige him. Her father volunteered at Horse Wise, so he knew that Dorothy and Nigel were coming to Pine Hollow. However, he told

Carole, he didn't know anything about tickets to the horse show and about the event that Nigel was participating in.

"It's called Gambler's Choice," Carole explained. "Each rider has a certain amount of time, maybe ninety seconds, to run the course. There are a lot of different jumps out there, and they can choose to go over any of them. The easy ones are worth like ten or twenty points. Harder ones are worth forty or fifty points. If they want, they can just go over the easy jumps again and again, but if they want to win, they have to take chances—gamble, see!"

Her father nodded. She went on, "So then there's the monster jump. I think they call it The Joker. It's worth a lot of points. But if you try it and knock it down, that many points are deducted from your score. High score wins. It's a very exciting event. I've never seen it, but I've always wanted to. I've read about it. I really hope we can go."

"Why wouldn't you be able to go?" Colonel Hanson asked.

"Well, Max said he's got so much work to do, he doesn't even know if he'll have time to get us tickets. See, Dad, running a stable isn't easy. There are always horses to take care of and riders to please. And then, if one horse gets sick, you have to worry about that.

Then there's the equipment that has to be taken care of and classes that are scheduled and special events that come up. And repairs. There are constant repairs. If it's not the stable, it's the fencing, and if it's not the fencing, it's the feed shed. And all the tack that has to be kept in good shape, cleaned, and polished. It's a lot of work."

"Are you sure you want to do this for a living?" the colonel asked.

"Oh, yes," Carole said. "And a lot more, too! No question about it. I love every minute of it."

"I guess I know that. Sometimes I have the feeling that if it weren't for the fact that occasionally you need to eat a meal—other than a sundae—and change your clothes, you'd be happy to live at Pine Hollow."

"Only if you were there, too," Carole assured him.

He smiled at her. The two of them were very close. Carole was sure she had the most wonderful father in the whole world, most of the time. They had always been close to one another, but since the death of Carole's mother a few years earlier, they'd become even closer.

The phone rang then. Colonel Hanson answered it.

"Oh, hi," he said when he knew who the caller was.

"Yes . . . sure. Sounds good to me. Or that, too. Either, I think. Well, you could, I guess. I can ask her. Sure, a jacket would go with that. I don't remember the horse shirt. No, she's wearing sneakers."

Carole scrunched her forehead. She couldn't imagine whom her father was talking to or what he was talking about. She looked down at her feet. She was wearing sneakers, but how could that be connected?

"Jeans are too casual, definitely. But nobody would recognize you if you wore a skirt. . . ."

Stevie? It had to be Stevie. Then the whole call made at least some sense. Stevie loved Carole's father almost as much as Carole did. They had a lot in common, too. They shared the most awful old jokes— usually about elephants or grapes—and they loved music from the fifties. This wasn't the first time Stevie had wanted Colonel Hanson's opinion about clothes, either. Stevie had this idea that since Carole's father was a single man about town, he knew what looked good on young women. The colonel was flattered by this. Carole thought that was the real reason Stevie asked him.

"Right, Stevie. The blue goes well with your eyes. Oh, yes, I've always liked you in blue. But have I ever seen you in anything *but* blue? Jeans, I mean?" The colonel was quiet for a while then, nodding as he listened. He said "hmmmmm" occasionally. Carole waited patiently.

Finally her father handed her the phone. "It's Stevie, for you," he said. "She can't decide what to wear on Friday to the horse show."

Carole let out a breath of air. How could Stevie be concerned with what she was going to wear? The horses would never notice, and nobody else mattered at all! She took the phone.

"Hi, Stevie," she said. "Wear those blue slacks, the turtleneck shirt, and your blue skiing sweater. I have a pair of flats that will go with that. I think they're yours anyway. . . ."

5

THE GIRLS MET in the locker area of Pine Hollow right after school on Monday. For once they were all on time. There was a lot of work to do and not much time to do it.

"Here's the chart I made up," Lisa said, handing each of her friends a printout—the result of all her work over the weekend.

"As you'll see, there are jobs that can be done in one day, or really in just a few minutes, like checking the bales of hay for mold, and others that we will need to spread out over the whole five days because they're so big, like reorganizing the specialized riding clothes in the attic. We'll do some of that each day, okay?"

Stevie gaped at the enormous list and the elaborate chart in her hand. "Does anyone ever get time off for good behavior?" she asked.

"Of course," Carole sniffed. "That's what's going to happen Friday night. That's what we're working for here, and I don't think you should be joking about it."

"I'm not joking," Stevie said. "There's nothing funny about all the work Max expects us to do."

"Are you complaining?" Lisa asked. She was suspicious because of Stevie's recent history of getting her friends to help her do things she really should have done herself.

"Oh, no," Stevie said. "Really I'm not. That's not what I meant. What I meant was that there's so much work here that Max asked us to do that I hate to think how much more work he must have to do himself."

Neither Carole nor Lisa had thought about it that way. In fact, they had both been thinking more along the lines that they'd thought *Stevie* had been thinking —that Max seemed to expect an awful lot of them. They'd completely misjudged Stevie and found themselves a little embarrassed about it.

"Of course you're right," Carole said. "I guess I was only thinking about us—not about Max. Poor guy."

"Yeah," Lisa agreed. "But what are we going to do about it?"

Both Lisa and Carole looked to Stevie for an answer to that question. She had one.

"We're going to do everything he asked us—plus something."

"What something?"

"I don't know yet," Stevie said. "The idea, though, is that he needs our help and he's going to thank us by taking us to the horse show. We need to find a way to thank him for that."

"Something special," Carole said.

"Something *fun*," Stevie said. And when Stevie decided on fun, fun was what they were going to have. Her eyes gleamed, but she told her friends that she wasn't ready to decide exactly what extra thing they should do, so they might as well get to work.

Lisa went to check for mold on the older bales of hay. Carole and Stevie mixed a week's worth of regular grains for the stable horses and a week's worth of the special mix that Veronica diAngelo claimed the vet had prescribed for Garnet. Stevie wasn't convinced that the slight difference in grains that Veronica required actually made any difference. Carole reminded her that it wasn't their business to question Veronica's vet.

"Even if Saturday is April Fools' Day?" Stevie asked.

47

Carole groaned. "Oh, no!"

"What?"

"April Fools' Day again! I hate it. You always take it as such a challenge, and I spend most of the rest of the month getting you out of the hot water you dive into so easily on the first of the month!"

Stevie poured a bag of grain into the mixing bin. "Why, Carole. How could you say such a thing?"

"Easily," Carole said. "If I recall correctly, one year you replaced Mrs. Reg's reading glasses with another pair, and she spent the whole day looking as if she were playing a trombone. And then there was the time you moved all the horses into different stalls. Max wasn't too thrilled about that one. Oh, and it seems to me that Max was even less happy about the time you replaced the belt that goes with his breeches with one that was two inches shorter. He spent the whole day talking about diets. Then there was the gelatin-in-the-sink year—oh, yes, and the whoopie cushion under Mr. Martin's saddle. Was that the same year you put the rubber horse manure in Mrs. di-Angelo's Mercedes-Benz?"

Stevie stirred the grains together thoughtfully. "I think they were all the same year," she said. "The year before was when I—"

"Stop! I can't stand it," Carole said. "Your April

Fools' pranks have been nothing but trouble. You just can't get away with this stuff all the time, Stevie."

"Do you mean to tell me that you didn't like hearing Mrs. diAngelo scream like that?" Stevie asked.

Carole had to think for a minute. She could still recall the woman's hollering and her indignant outrage as she tried to imagine how a horse had actually gotten into her car to make the deposit. She'd yelled at Max and the stable hand, Red. She'd even yelled at Veronica. Then, when she'd discovered the manure was only rubber, she'd yelled at Stevie—knowing that only she would come up with something like that. Stevie hadn't minded at all.

"It was kind of fun," Carole admitted. "But you're not going to do it again, are you?"

"No, I don't think so," Stevie said. "This year I'm only going to do nice things."

Carole thought that sounded like a good idea. April Fools' Day and Stevie could be a pretty dangerous combination. She decided that she and Lisa might have to add "keep Stevie out of trouble" to their list of jobs for the week.

The next task they tackled was to look at the dress riding clothes that were stored in the attic of the house that Max and his mother, Mrs. Reg, shared. Max pulled the ladder down for them and showed them where the light switch was. Then he left them alone.

Carole was the first of the three girls to enter the attic, but she felt as if she were the first person to visit in a century. The March sunlight filtered through dingy glass windows and seemed to hold dust particles in suspension. There was a dry, stuffy smell to the place, but it wasn't unpleasant. It was as if the air had been as undisturbed as the trunks and dress racks that cluttered the room. Carole felt that she might be breathing the very same air that had filled the lungs of Max's grandfather.

The room was large but might have seemed bigger if it hadn't been for all the clothes that had been abandoned there haphazardly over the years. The floor around the ladder was circled by boxes that had obviously been shoved onto the floor of the attic without actually being stored.

Carole made a pathway among the cartons so her friends could join her. Lisa came up next and just looked around in silent awe. Stevie, on the other hand, had something to say.

"Wow."

"Yeah," Carole agreed.

"We get to look in all these boxes!" said Stevie. Stevie was a very curious person. A closed box had always been a challenge to her. Now, however, as she took in the enormity of the task, she began to realize that this job might challenge the limits of even her curiosity.

"Okay, now, here's what we should do," said Lisa. Carole and Stevie listened up. Lisa always seemed to know how to tackle a big task. "We should begin by sorting. I think our categories are going to be (1) stuff to be thrown out; (2) stuff to be given away; (3) antique and historical clothes to be stored and put away; (4) specialty clothes to be stored for special occasions; and (5) everyday riding clothes that ought to be used. Now, for starters, let's move all the car—Stevie? What are you doing?"

Even in the face of all of Lisa's logic and organization, Stevie couldn't contain herself. She'd opened the nearest box and was down on her knees pawing through its contents.

"You won't believe this stuff, guys!" she said excitedly. "I mean, look at this!"

The next thing Carole and Lisa knew, Stevie had on a new hat. It was a pearl-gray bowler, and it looked very funny on her, especially because it was too big and pushed her ears out at odd angles from her head.

"The latest fashion!" Lisa said, giggling.

"Well, here's one for you," Stevie said, tossing a

black flat-topped hat at Lisa. It looked like a top hat, cut short.

Then she reached in farther and pulled out another top hat. This one she gave to Carole. While Carole put it on, Stevie went back into the box and began pulling out the clothes that went with the hats.

"These are for saddle-seat equitation," Carole informed her friends, confirming their suspicions that Carole knew everything there was to know about horses. "You remember, don't you? At the horse show in New York, we saw classes with the saddlebreds?"

The girls did remember then. Saddlebreds were the horses that had been trained to move with their front feet lifting high off the ground. They pranced more than walked. Their riders wore fancy old-fashioned clothes. The coats were cut long, almost like skirts.

"The clothes were cool, but I didn't much like the way the horses moved," Lisa said. "It just didn't look natural to me."

"I don't think it *is* natural," Stevie agreed. "They have to do a lot of training with those horses, and it can't be much fun. Remember how nervous the animals were when we saw them?"

Lisa did remember. The slightest movement around the saddlebreds would elicit a strong reaction, as if the horses were afraid of everything.

"I didn't know Max ever had saddlebreds around here," she said.

"I don't know that he did," Stevie said. "But he's got some clothes for them—and I think we're going to have to try them on to be sure they're in good enough condition that they should be kept instead of thrown away."

Carole and Lisa certainly agreed with that. In a flash, all three girls were reaching for outfits to try on. They had to open six more cartons before they found shirts, vests, ties, and boots to go with the hats they'd started with, but it was clearly worth it. Within minutes they'd put on not only clothes, but personalities.

"Milady, would you care to take a hack in the park this afternoon?" Stevie asked, removing her hat and bowing formally to Carole.

Carole found herself transformed into a Southern belle. "Why, I declare, I do think I would!" she said, batting her eyelashes at the handsome squire she imagined in the baggy clothes Stevie wore. "But only if mah little sistah Lillibelle can join us."

Stevie looked at Lisa, who cocked her hat down over her face shyly. "Why, of co'se Miz Lillibelle may join us!" she said.

"You want li'l ole me?" Lisa asked. She was having trouble, though. In the first place, the pants she wore were too big, so she had to hold them up with one hand. Her other problem was keeping from laughing because she felt so silly. Finally she couldn't hold it in. Carole and Stevie joined in the laughter. Then Stevie located an old mirror. The three of them took turns looking at themselves in the dingy glass.

Much to Lisa's surprise, she didn't look as silly in the mirror as she'd felt dressing in the clothes. Although the pants were too big and the whole outfit ridiculously formal, she looked good, and so did her friends.

"We look like show riders," Carole said, admiring her own reflection.

"Either that or band leaders," Stevie agreed.

"Not bad," said Lisa. "Not bad."

"But maybe there's better around," Stevie said, slipping out of her outfit. "Let's try some more boxes."

A part of Lisa told herself that this was silly. They didn't have time to try on clothes and play. There was too much work to be done. Another part of her told herself that, after all, they did have to open all the boxes so that they could sort all the contents. And the best way to be sure what the contents were was to try on the clothes themselves. That was the part of her that won the argument.

The girls couldn't believe all the things they found. There was an almost infinite variety of riding pants, shirts, ties, vests, and jackets. They even found a selection of culottes for women riders. Those were pants designed to look like skirts that could be used to ride sidesaddle.

Clothes began flying all over the attic.

"Here, try this on!"

"Look at this!"

"Eeowww—did someone actually *wear* this?"

"Riding a horse???"

"Look at how this vest hangs down below the jacket!"

"And how the jacket hangs down below everything!"

"It's called a shad-belly."

"Isn't it called tails?"

"No, shad-belly."

"Weird."

Stevie began dressing Carole up in a pearl-gray outfit with one of the large split skirts. There was a ruffly white blouse that went under the jacket. She wasn't sure it was the blouse that was originally intended to go under the jacket, but it looked nice. She found some gray boots that matched and a white riding crop. She ransacked three more boxes in search of accessories. She was looking for a pair of white gloves. What she found, however, was a box of camping gear, and though it didn't have white gloves, it did have white mosquito netting.

"Just the thing," she declared. With that, she lifted the netting up over Carole's formally clad head, and as it settled on her, all three girls were overwhelmed with the image, for there, standing in front of a dingy mirror in a dusty attic, wearing an old-fashioned riding outfit, was a bride. Carole looked as if she were completely ready to ride down the aisle to meet up with the man of her dreams.

"Look at that!" said Lisa.

"What inspiration!" said Stevie.

Carole immediately sensed something in Stevie's tone of voice. "Inspiration?" she asked.

"Sure," said Stevie. "We can have a wedding!"

"We're missing only two things," Lisa commented. "The bride and the groom."

"No, we've got them already. The new stallion is the groom and Delilah is the bride! It's going to be great. We can do it on Saturday, *after* the horse show. You can ride Delilah, wearing that outfit—you might want to consider adding a string of pearls somewhere, though—and then one of us can wear the outfit I had on before—you know, the Southern-gentleman thing

—and that person can lead the stallion, and then the other one can be the justice of the peace."

"Just where is this going to take place?" Carole asked.

"In the paddock," Stevie said quickly. Then she had another idea. "Or maybe we'll think of someplace more romantic. Anyway, we can ask all the members of Horse Wise to bring food. We can make it a surprise for them, too. You know, just the three of us will be in on it, so everybody will be bowled over. It is, after all, The Day—I mean April Fools'—and it's the kind of joke that's fun and nobody gets hurt, and that's the kind you're always wanting me to think up."

Carole had a couple of questions she wanted to ask Stevie right then, like if she was totally out of her mind and how they could possibly plan a whole party, to say nothing of a wedding, in four days when they had a whole lot of other things that had to be done— but there was no stopping Stevie. Her mind was totally engaged and her mouth was just as active.

". . . then there's the music. I guess we'll just have to use a battery-powered tape deck. I can probably borrow my brother's, though he may kill me if anything happens to it, but he won't even notice, since I think he's going away this weekend. I'd better borrow it Thursday so he won't even think of taking it with him on Friday. What music? I mean, we're going to have to have classical stuff for the ceremony—oh, the ceremony, I guess I'm going to have to write that. Or better still, Lisa, you write it. You're good at writing. . . ."

Lisa and Carole began sorting some of the clothes they'd taken out of boxes, listening to Stevie's chatter as they worked. When Stevie was this enthusiastic about a plan, it usually turned out pretty well. Usually.

6

By the time riding class started on Tuesday, Stevie had everyone thoroughly confused. She'd decided that the "wedding" for Delilah and the stallion should be a surprise not only for Max, but for everyone. However, in order to get everyone to work on it, she had to give them a reason.

"It's Max's birthday, and we need somebody to bring punch," she said to Meg Durham. "Can you do that?"

Meg agreed.

She asked Veronica diAngelo to bake the cake, not because she thought Veronica would actually bake it, but because she suspected that Veronica's cook would do a better job than most of the students.

"White, it has to be white," Stevie said.

"Why? I thought Max liked chocolate cake the best."

"Maybe," said Stevie, thinking fast. "But all I have is white candles—oh, and by the way, don't write anything on the cake."

As usual, Veronica was being contrary. "White candles go just fine on a chocolate cake, and what's wrong with writing 'Happy Birthday Max'?"

"My white candles won't go on a chocolate cake, and don't write anything on it because I told you so."

Stevie could be contrary, too.

With only ten minutes to spare before class started, she'd gotten one girl to offer to bring streamers (light blue, not white, but that would be good enough, Stevie figured), another to make a festive white satin bow, and one of the boys agreed to bring his entire collection of opera music tapes because Stevie thought that would mean that somewhere in there they'd find the wedding march from *Lohengrin*.

"Why do you want opera?" he'd asked. "I think Max likes rhythm and blues."

"He'll change his mind soon enough," Stevie had answered.

April agreed to bring glasses; Polly offered napkins and paper plates. Betsy Cavanaugh said she could bring ginger ale, but preferred to bring cola. Stevie wanted ginger ale because it looked like champagne. She stuck to her guns. Betsy had definitely met her match in Stevie and agreed. Ginger ale it was. Adam Levine said his parents had lots of folding chairs, and Joe Novick agreed to help set them up, but neither of them thought it was a very good idea to have them all in rows.

"How can we have a party that way?" Joe asked.

"Trust me, we can," Stevie said. "Besides, we may move them again. But to start, I want them here." She pointed to the place where she intended to have the audience for the wedding. "With an aisle."

"Aye, aye, ma'am," Joe said. Almost everybody, except Veronica, had learned that it was usually easier to agree with Stevie than to argue with her.

"Stevie!" That was Max. "Class starts in five minutes, and I just saw that Topside isn't even tacked up!"

That was bad news. It took from ten to fifteen minutes to tack up a horse properly. Max was never happy when his students were late for class, especially when the reason appeared to be because they were just chatting with the other students.

"I'll be ready, Max. I promise!"

She flew. Stevie didn't have a second to waste. There was no point in planning a wonderful party for Max when he would be too angry at her to enjoy it— even a nice April Fools' horses' wedding party. She was going to have to work fast, and she was going to need help.

Lisa and Carole saw that and pitched in, as usual. Lisa brought the saddle and Carole carried the bridle. Stevie gave Topside a quick brushing, and then all three of them put on his tack. He'd never had so much attention from so many people all at once in his whole life. He loved every second of it. At the very moment the PA system crackled out the announcement that class was beginning, Stevie was ready to mount up and enter the ring.

"Stevie, you are amazing," Max remarked as she and Topside walked into the class—on time.

"It's a miracle," she joked.

"It's a miracle that you can get your friends to help you with your work all the time," he said. Giggles and smirks emerged from almost everybody in the class because Max didn't have half an idea of how true his statement was. He looked around curiously and shrugged.

"Line up in the middle of the ring," he announced. Class began.

Stevie soon realized that Max may have shrugged off her near lateness, but he was clearly irritated with her, because he watched her like a hawk through the class.

"Heels down!" he ordered. She put them down. "And keep your knees in."

"They are in."

"Not enough," he barked. "And sit up straight. Stop wiggling your hands around!"

Stevie tried very hard to do everything he told her. Certainly everything he said was designed to improve her riding form, but she'd thought she already had these basics down pat.

"Now keep your lower legs perpendicular to the ground!"

"Yes, Max," she said. There was a part of her that wanted to growl at him. She didn't think he was really being fair. After all, Anna McWhirter wasn't riding nearly as well as she was, and Max wasn't saying anything to Anna, but she decided it wouldn't be a good idea to get into an argument with him. It might make her change her mind about having the mock wedding on Saturday if she got too angry with him, and she didn't want anything to interfere with that.

"And eyes straight ahead!"

"Yes, Max," she managed to say through clenched teeth.

As class drew to a close and the riders were walking their horses around the ring to cool them down, Max talked about the visitors they were going to have on Saturday.

That was when he told the rest of the students about the new stallion and what it would mean to Pine Hollow. The riders were all as excited as The Saddle Club was. They agreed that there was nothing nicer than the idea that there would be the patter of little hooves around Pine Hollow.

Max asked for some help after class setting up the paddock where the stallion, Geronimo, would spend most of his time. Some of the ground had become very uneven, and he wanted to smooth it out.

The Saddle Club had other chores to do from Max's list, but he seemed to expect them to pitch in on this one as well. Stevie told Max she couldn't stay. She had to get to a dentist appointment.

Lisa and Carole looked at one another. They knew that wasn't true.

"I've got to get to the shopping center and pick up some things for Saturday," Stevie whispered to Carole. And before Carole could point out that they all could go to the shopping center together *after* helping

Max and after doing some more work in the attic, Stevie was gone.

"She's so busy," Lisa said.

"And so are we," Carole commented. She took the shovel Max handed her and followed the wheelbarrow full of dirt to the paddock. Lisa carried a rake.

"Our goals are all the same," Lisa reminded Carole. "We need to get all this work done *and* have a special treat for Max."

"Why does it seem unfair that she does the fun stuff like shopping, and you and I end up spreading dirt around a lumpy paddock?"

Lisa thought about this for a minute. Much as she wanted to defend Stevie, Carole did have a point. On the other hand, there were things to be done at the shopping center, and the whole Saddle Club couldn't duck out of the chore Max had given all the riders, or it would look suspicious. At Pine Hollow, everybody pitched in.

"Stevie's really good at finding great stuff to buy at the shopping center," Lisa said. "And remember the thrift shop that's just opened up there? I bet there's a ton of really wonderful things."

Carole thought about it, too. "You're right," she said finally. "It took Stevie to think of mosquito netting as a bridal veil. She'll see all kinds of possibilities there where you and I would only see junk."

"Yeah," Lisa said, hefting her rake with renewed vigor.

"I just wish we were there to see those possibilities with her," Carole said.

"Yeah," Lisa agreed.

Red O'Malley dumped the first load of earth into the paddock then, and the girls began the task of spreading it out evenly. It required some attention and some strength. They stopped thinking about Stevie for a while.

7

"ALL RIGHT NOW, smile for the photographer," Stevie instructed Lisa and Carole.

Lisa groaned and Carole grimaced.

"That's not right at all," Stevie said. "Remember, the pictures that will be taken at the actual wedding are going to be a permanent reminder of this wonderful day. Geronimo and Delilah will be able to look at them for years—show them to their grandchildren!"

"This is supposed to be a *rehearsal*!" Lisa said, exasperated.

"For the real thing," Stevie persisted.

It was Wednesday afternoon, after school. The three girls had met at Pine Hollow as soon as they could excuse themselves from their classes—and that was pretty fast. Although there were a lot of chores listed on Lisa's printout for today, Stevie had convinced the girls that the best way to prepare for some hard work was to have a relaxing trail ride. She'd then managed to turn it into a wedding rehearsal, and it wasn't going very well, except in Stevie's eyes.

Carole was riding Starlight and Lisa was riding Delilah. She'd always wanted to try the beautiful mare and found her to be as lovely a horse as she'd dreamed. She wasn't surprised by how much Judge Gavin enjoyed riding her.

"I used to ride her before she foaled," Carole said. "I would have been glad to ride her again, except that Dad gave me Starlight."

"Enough talk about horses," Stevie interrupted. "Let's get back to the wedding. All right, now, Lisa and Carole, you two will ride down the aisle. . . ."

Stevie was being just about impossible, as only Stevie could be. Most of the time her "impossible" side was offset by her own wonderful mischievousness, and it was fun. Sometimes, however, her "impossible" side was merely bossy. That's what it was now. Stevie was obsessed with this wedding, and though Carole and Lisa suspected the whole thing would, in fact, end up being fun, for now it was very hard work. The hardest part was keeping from yelling at Stevie.

"No, no," Stevie spoke sharply. "You've got to have the horses walk *together*."

"They are together," Lisa said.

"No, I mean they have to step at the same time!"

"Stevie!" Carole said. "That's a very difficult technique!"

"Well, that's why we're practicing."

Stevie had everything figured out. The two "bridesmaids" would enter the "chapel," with Lisa on Delilah and Carole on Starlight. Since Geronimo was a stallion and not really suitable as a saddle horse for a young rider, the "chapel" would be situated right next to his paddock. He'd be curious about all the goings-on, Stevie assured her friends, and he'd come right up to the corner of the paddock, where he'd be in the perfect position to be "wed" to Delilah.

"It's going to be a beautiful wedding," Stevie said, practically sighing in anticipation. "There won't be a dry eye in the house!" She paused, and then she got another idea. "Hesitation step. Can you do a hesitation step?"

That was a form of walking in a processional where the walker paused before bringing the back leg forward. It was a little tricky when a person was walking and was considered an advanced feat in dressage riding. There was no way either Carole or Lisa could do that. They said as much to Stevie.

"Well, *try* anyway, won't you? I mean, wouldn't it be wonderful?"

"Stevie!" Lisa said, finally reduced to yelling at her friend.

"Is something wrong?" Stevie asked. She was apparently totally unaware of the fact that she was being more than a little annoying.

"We'll try," Carole said, sighing.

The two girls returned to the imaginary entrance to the imaginary chapel and tried again.

This time, though, they could not in any way make their horses walk with a hesitation step, they did, by chance, have them walking and stepping at the same time. They expected Stevie to appreciate that.

"Smile," Stevie said. "Really big smiles!"

"I'm going to throttle her," Lisa muttered under her breath.

"You're going to have to beat me to it," said Carole.

"I said smile! Look happy!"

"I'm out of here," Lisa said, turning Delilah sharply to the right. Carole followed.

"What are you doing? You're supposed to be coming down the aisle! I think the aisle ought to be straight, but maybe it would be interesting if it wound around a little bit, but not too much. . . ."

Stevie went on thinking out loud, barely noticing what her two friends were doing. She was definitely missing the point. She had a rebellion on her hands, and the mutineers intended to make it clear that they were tired of being told exactly what to do all the time, especially when it didn't make any sense.

Carole and Lisa trotted their horses away from Stevie's fantasy chapel. They weren't really angry with Stevie, they just had to make their point that they didn't want to be bossed around. The best way to do that seemed to be to stop doing what she told them.

It was a nice day, fresh and warm for the end of March—more like summer than spring. The horses paused in the middle of a clump of spring wildflowers. Delilah took a bite of fresh green grass, including a few yellow blossoms.

"She's always loved flowers," Carole observed. "They must taste good."

"She reminds me of Ferdinand, the bull who liked to smell the flowers."

"That gives me an idea," Carole said. "I think I know how we can make our point to Stevie." With that she dismounted, walked Starlight over to a nearby fence, where she secured his reins, and then returned to Lisa and the flower patch. "Let's be Ferdinand ourselves."

Lisa got the idea. She took Delilah over to where Starlight was, and then she joined Carole. The two of them sat in the middle of the flower patch. Lisa plucked a yellow flower and then a white one. She twined their stems together and then picked another yellow. She added that to the chain.

"How'd you do that?" Carole asked. Lisa showed her.

"It's called a daisy chain," Lisa said. "But, of course, you can do it with any flower at all."

Carole picked a couple of flowers and, after a couple of attempts, figured out how to do it herself. It was kind of fun.

When Lisa's chain was about a foot long, she drew the ends together to make a circle and then put it on top of her riding hat.

Carole smiled and hurried to finish her own. The rebellion was turning out to be kind of fun. She found that she didn't mind if they never got back to Stevie's wedding rehearsal. They'd just sit there and weave flowers all day long.

"Nice!" said Stevie. "I like it! I thought you two were giving up on me, but look at you! You've figured out how to get flowers into our wedding. Great!"

Lisa and Carole looked at one another. They couldn't help laughing. Stevie was so deeply embroiled in planning the wedding that she couldn't even tell when they were rebelling! If that was the case, there was clearly no point in doing it. Stevie was being Stevie, and after all, she was their best friend, even if she was sometimes just a tiny little bit annoying.

"Yes," Carole said finally. "We just knew there was something else we'd have to do to make this wedding perfect. Besides—we don't have enough to do to keep us busy for the next few days, so we decided to weave flowers together. Like it?"

"I love it!" Stevie said. "If we pick the flowers this afternoon right before we go back to Pine Hollow, then we can keep them fresh in the old refrigerator off the rec room at my house where we keep sodas cold. Then, maybe on Friday night after the horse show, or Saturday morning, we can do the weaving. Is it hard to learn to do? I hope not, because it looks just wonderful. You know, if we get enough flowers, we could make a whole bower. Do you think we could cover that grape arbor? If we could, then we could have the whole wedding right there. It's so pretty, and it's next to Geronimo's paddock. Imagine how nice it would look covered with flowers. . . ."

Lisa and Carole shook their heads, then remounted and worked on their wedding processional again and again until she was satisfied. After that the girls picked all the flowers they could carry and returned to Pine Hollow, where there were just a few little tasks for them to do.

Lisa checked the list. According to her schedule, this was the day they were supposed to give Geronimo's new stall a thorough cleaning and prepare it for him. They were also supposed to clean three more saddles; sort through a collection of bits and arrange them by size; sort through the riding hats that Max kept for riders who didn't have one of their own and hang them by size; and spend some more time in the attic with the boxes of clothes.

And that didn't even count any of the things that Stevie might still want them to do for the "wedding."

The girls hurried back to the stable, though it wasn't easy to ride quickly with armfuls of flowers, especially when they didn't want Max or Mrs. Reg or anybody, really, to see all the blossoms. Then, while Lisa and Carole untacked all three horses and groomed them, Stevie ran the flowers over to her house to put them in the refrigerator there, promising she'd be back to help as quickly as possible.

When Carole and Lisa finished with their own

horses and met in Topside's stall to take care of Stevie's horse, it occurred to them that, once again, they seemed to be doing something that was really Stevie's responsibility. They didn't think about that for long, however, because just as they were putting away Stevie's grooming bucket, she reappeared, ready, willing, and able to clean out Geronimo's stall, polish saddles, sort through bits, and return to the attic. Of course, before she did all that, she had to make a few phone calls to be sure everybody knew what they were supposed to bring on Saturday.

Lisa and Carole picked up pitchforks. Stevie picked up the phone.

8

By the time Friday arrived, the girls thought they would never finish everything Max had asked them to do. They'd spent more time than they probably had to working on the clothes in the attic, because it was so much fun. They'd also spent less time than they probably ought to cleaning tack, because it wasn't any fun at all. But many of the jobs they were doing for Max were close enough to complete for them to hope Max would let them go to the horse show.

The only other problem, then, was Stevie. She wasn't going to let them get away so easily. At Stevie's insistence, they met at Pine Hollow at seven-thirty on Friday morning, before school.

"What are we doing here?" Lisa asked.

"We are having a rehearsal," Stevie said.

"We already had a rehearsal," Carole reminded her.

"We haven't had a rehearsal at the actual chapel," Stevie said.

"This is a chapel?" asked Lisa. She looked around the paddock, still misty in the cool of the early spring morning. Behind her stood the grape arbor that would serve as a bower for the bridal couple.

"It will be," Stevie assured her friends. "If you guys finish all the work with the flowers."

That was a pointed reminder that there was a lot left to be done, even after they'd finished the rehearsal.

"Now everything has to be just perfect," Stevie said. Her voice assumed the tone of a bridal consultant, gushing so that the bride's mother wouldn't dare to object to how much money was being spent on the perfection. In this case, however, money wasn't really the issue. Work was.

"It's going to be really nice," Carole said, mustering a bit of enthusiasm.

"In my experience," Stevie went on in her consultant's voice, "it's the little touches that make the wedding a success. So the first thing you two have to do is tack up the horses and be sure that you do fit together under the arbor. The processional is very important, and I want you to be able to ride side by side."

"Okay," Lisa agreed. It was just easier to go along.

While Lisa and Carole were tacking up their horses, Stevie checked her list to see what things they would have to do that night after the horse show. They were having a sleepover at her house.

There was still a lot of work to do on the hors d'oeuvres for the party. For a people wedding, you could have just people food, but for this one, she'd had to make some concessions. She'd added carrots and apples to the menu. This wasn't the first time she'd done that, either. When she'd produced a retirement party for Pepper, another horse at Pine Hollow, the food had included goodies for *all* the guests, especially the guest of honor. This time she wanted to be sure there were some sugar lumps. She thought her mother had some in the house. Then she decided they'd look really wonderful if they could add just a touch of food coloring—colors that would match the color scheme of the wedding itself. Since the crepe paper was going to be blue, the sugar lumps could also be blue. What a great idea, she thought, jotting that down on her list of "To Do's" right next to slicing apples. They'd have a very busy night, indeed, and then, tomorrow, they'd have a wonderful party.

"Okay, here we are," Carole announced.

It didn't take very long then. Stevie had the two of them ride under the grape arbor, side by side. It was just a little bit low for them, but as long as they ducked, ever so slightly, there was no problem. They fit.

"It's going to look *lovely*," Stevie said.

"She's gushing again," Lisa remarked.

"Just like a mother of the bride," Carole said.

Stevie knew it was true. The fact was that she did feel like the mother of the bride. She was taking a very personal attitude toward this party. She'd done some work on the other chores her friends had completed this week, but most of her attention, and all of her heart, was invested in the success of this, her ultimate April Fools' joke. She didn't want to admit it to her friends, but one of the reasons this was true was that she had decided not to play any other April Fools' jokes on anybody this year. Not even her brothers. That had been a very difficult decision for Stevie, who considered her brothers to be perfect targets of April Fools' jokes. The fact was that she *wanted* to play jokes on them all year round, but the only time she stood a chance of getting away with it was on

April Fools' Day. That meant that this "wedding" was a big sacrifice for her. She wanted it to count. She was sure it would.

Stevie looked at her watch. It was almost eight o'clock, and that meant it was time for them to untack the horses and hurry to school. Fortunately, their schools were all within easy walking distance of Pine Hollow, so they'd probably be on time. There were four other things Stevie had wanted to get done, but they were out of the question. At her school, tardiness meant detention, and this was no day for detention. There was too much to do.

"Hurry up!" she chided Carole and Lisa, who gave her very dirty looks.

THAT AFTERNOON AT Pine Hollow, there was no question of wedding rehearsals. There were too many people around, and one of them, Max Regnery, would immediately know something was up. The girls worked instead on trying to complete as many of the jobs he'd given them as they could.

Lisa was given the job of sorting out the various extra stirrups that had been collecting in a corner of the tack room. She was supposed to make them into pairs, whenever possible, and fasten the pairs together with a twister. She found the task was very similar to sorting socks out of a load of wash. She enjoyed it every bit as much.

"Is this close enough?" she asked, holding up a slight mismatch.

"No," Stevie and Carole said in a single voice. Lisa looked again.

Carole's job was to sort out the medicine cabinet. It seemed that Max had collected hundreds of bottles of many different kinds of medicines for his horses. Carole knew that veterinary medicine was very different from human medicine in many ways. One of the ways was that medicines could be administered by owners and the prescriptions weren't handled the way human prescriptions were. Max had a large collection, so that if Pine Hollow's vet, Judy Barker, prescribed a common medicine, chances were that Max had it on hand —if he could find it. He'd allowed his medicine chest to get into a frightful state. The biggest problem, Carole found, was that a lot of the medicines had passed their expiration dates and had probably lost strength. There would be no way of telling what proper doses would be. Carole began throwing out all the out-of-date medicines. It took her a while to figure out how to organize the ones that remained. Finally she decided on alphabetical order. It was, at least, order.

Stevie's job was to dust all of the saddles in the tack

room. That was instead of polishing them all, which is what Max had asked them to do. Most of them were actually pretty clean, and a dusting made them look cleaner. It wasn't quite what Max had in mind, but since the afternoon was almost over, it was going to be all they had time for.

"Nice job," Max said, walking past the tack room. Stevie smiled. Then she realized that she should take the opportunity to ask him if he'd actually been able to get tickets for them for the horse show.

"Uh, Max," she began. He stopped and returned to the tack room. "Did you have time to call—"

His mind seemed to be on something else, though. He interrupted her, asking, "Weren't you supposed to polish all those saddles instead of just dusting them?"

Stevie gulped. "I'm just about to," she assured him. "Wanted to make sure they were dust free first."

"Sure," he said, but he didn't sound as if he believed her. Before she had a chance to protest her innocence, he turned and left the tack room. Stevie picked up the tin of saddle soap. A couple of the saddles really were dirty. If she just soaped them, that would probably be good enough. She hoped so, anyway.

Lisa and Carole joined Stevie in the tack room and each picked up a sponge and pitched in. They didn't like the idea that Max had noticed their glaring omission.

Lisa grimaced as she polished. "I have to say, though, that maybe if we hadn't been spending quite so much time on the party for tomorrow, we might have gotten more of these chores done."

"But the whole idea of the wedding is to thank Max for all he's done," Stevie reminded her friends.

"Maybe," Carole said. "But aren't we sort of thanking him by doing all this work?"

"It's been a *lot* of work," Lisa added.

"Yes, it has," Stevie agreed. "And Max is just going to *love* it. Tomorrow, while we're having a blast at the wedding, you will forget all the hard things we've done, and all you'll remember is how much fun we're going to have. It'll be the best April Fools' Day of all."

"And there *have* been a number of memorable ones," Carole mused.

"Yeah," Stevie said wistfully. Her friends thought she was probably remembering the horse-manure episode again. They didn't think that was anything to be wistful about. Perhaps it was a lucky thing that Stevie had been so busy with this nice April Fools' prank that she hadn't had time to do any other ones.

"I guess you're right," Lisa said at last. "It'll be worth it."

"Girls?" It was Max. He was standing at the door of the tack room. They were worried that he might have overheard some of their conversation, but he seemed to have something else on his mind. "Are you still working? Shouldn't you be home eating dinner and changing your clothes? We're going to have to leave here before seven tonight to be sure to get to the horse show on time. You are planning on coming, aren't you?"

THE MINUTE THE girls entered the arena, they could feel the excitement of the horse show. All around them, spectators hurried to their seats.

"Look, there's a man in a tuxedo!" Lisa whispered to Carole.

"And look what his wife's wearing!" Stevie said, gawking at the full-length evening gown the woman had on. "Is this a dance, or what? Are we in the right place?" She looked down at her own very nice blue outfit, but it just didn't match up to the woman's gown.

"No, it's just that it's traditional for some people to dress up at the horse show."

"We're not traditional?" Stevie asked.

"We're the *new* tradition," Lisa explained. "Casual dress."

Then Stevie looked around again. This time she noticed that there were a lot more blue jeans than evening gowns. She smiled.

"Which way?" Carole asked, eager to get past the crowds of people and into the crowds of horses.

Max checked their tickets. "This way." He pointed to the left.

The girls, Max, and Mrs. Reg made their way through the gate, up an escalator, along a hallway, through a tunnel, and into the arena itself.

"Here? We sit *here?*" Stevie asked as they located their seats. She was expressing the surprise and excitement all three girls felt when they realized how good their seats were. They were practically *in* the ring. "Shouldn't we be climbing up some stairs, or sitting behind a pole or something?"

"No, this is where we're sitting," Max assured her. "And don't worry. Mother and I aren't dressed any fancier than you girls are."

Stevie sat down. She didn't sit for long, though, because as soon as they'd all settled into their seats, Dorothy DeSoto showed up. She was in work clothes since one of the horses she trained was competing tonight. That put Stevie totally at ease. Apparently you could wear anything at the horse show, and the more casually you were dressed, the more important you obviously were!

Dorothy had big hugs for Max and Mrs. Reg and for the whole Saddle Club.

"I'm so glad you could all come tonight!" she said. "This is one of my favorite nights of the horse show. It's going to be great." She glanced at her watch. "I've got to get back to work," she said. "But would any of you, say for instance some of the young riders here, like to come with me?"

"You mean like backstage?" Carole asked.

"That's where I'm headed," Dorothy said. "You might miss the first class, which is a saddlebred class, but you will get a special flavor of the show."

Max cleared his throat. "You mean you're willing to take a chance and let these three wild things loose with all those horses?"

"Sure," said Dorothy. "I might even put them to work, but more likely I'll just introduce them to Nigel. I've been telling him a lot about these girls."

"Uh-oh," said Stevie. "Where's the nearest exit?"

"This way," Dorothy said, leading them all through the gate into the backstage area of the arena.

The girls had been backstage at a horse show once

before, in New York. This was a very different place, though. It was much more spacious and comfortable. That was because in the middle of New York City, hundreds of horses had to be housed in a very small indoor area. This arena had more room, both inside and out, for the horses. They had an outdoor warm-up ring, as well as an indoor one. The warm-up ring in New York had been no larger than an average living room.

Dorothy walked past a warm-up ring, straight to the stabling area. Each stable had its own section where its horses were kept. Many competitors just had one stall. Some had five, six, or more, and their area would include not just a space for the trunk that held the horse's tack and grooming gear, but a whole miniature tack room.

Lisa's eyes couldn't take it all in. It seemed that every time they turned another corner (and there were plenty of those), somebody else was saying, "Hi, Dorothy. How's it going?" or "Have you seen Janice?" or "Good luck!" or "Did I already tell you Jack and I will be at the wedding?"

Dorothy knew everybody there, and everybody there liked her. It made the girls feel all the more important.

Then Dorothy stopped. She was at a large stabling

area that seemed to be covered with red, white, and blue bunting. At first Lisa thought it was American, but then she realized that everybody there was talking with a decidedly different accent, and then it occurred to her that England's colors were red, white, and blue, too.

"Nigel, here they are," Dorothy said. "This is Carole, Stevie, and Lisa—better known as The Saddle Club."

"Ah, the American girls who ride at Max's stable!" Nigel said. "And Dorothy told me something of your adventures in New York—something about a movie star who needed riding lessons?"

"That's right," Carole said, offering her hand. Lisa was glad Carole had spoken because she didn't think she would be able to. Nigel Hawthorne was the most impressive person she'd ever seen. He was very tall and slender. He had strong features, wide-set dark brown eyes, a fine nose, an even mouth, and impeccably combed hair. In fact, she would have been downright scared of him if it weren't for his wonderful, warm smile. He shook Carole's hand and then Stevie's and Lisa's in turn. Lisa found herself relaxing a little just because of his smile.

"I suppose it wasn't really me you wanted to meet, though, was it? It was my horse, right?"

"Well, we do love horses," Stevie said.

"Then come right this way."

Dorothy excused herself to go be with the horse she'd been training, saying she'd meet them all back at the seats. The girls followed Nigel.

The British Equestrian Team had four members at the horse show. They were competing in a number of events, including the Gambler's Choice, which would be this evening. Nigel explained that the team had more members, it was just that the alternates weren't needed now for this show.

The horses were all stabled in stalls next to one another, and two of the other riders were there as well. Nigel introduced the girls to his teammates, Camilla Wentworth and Alastair Brown. Then they met their horses.

The horses that Max kept at Pine Hollow were pretty good animals. Some of them were even quite valuable. But the girls didn't think they had ever seen such beautiful and valuable horses all in one place as they were looking at right then and there.

Camilla Wentworth was having a problem with her horse, Elementary, and she wanted Nigel's help.

"He's been acting up, very frisky," she said.

"Isn't that good?" Carole asked. It had always been her impression that when a horse was lively and fresh

—frisky—that was a good sign and boded well for a top performance.

"Not necessarily," Nigel said. "And not in this horse. Elementary is a very staid and steady performer. What's significant here is that his behavior is *different*."

That made sense. Carole and her friends watched while Nigel and Camilla examined Elementary carefully. They checked his basic health, temperature, pulse, and rate of breathing. Everything seemed normal. He wasn't showing any signs of lameness or swelling in his legs, and there were no tender areas on him that they could detect. They couldn't find any reason for a change in behavior patterns.

"I don't know," Nigel said, shrugging. "Carole could be right. Whatever it is, if it's anything at all, it could just help his performance."

"I hope you're right," Camilla said, but she eyed her horse doubtfully. She gave him a couple of pats on his neck and rubbed his cheek. He nuzzled her neck. "I guess he does seem fine," she said. Nobody could not think her horse was fine when he was in the process of tickling her neck! Camilla decided to walk Elementary around one of the warm-up rings, just to be sure. She snapped a lead on him and took him out of his stall. His motion seemed totally fluid and flawless.

Carole and her friends couldn't imagine that there was actually anything wrong with him.

Nearby, a groom was working to make Nigel's horse's coat shiny and perfect. The Saddle Club always prided themselves on being able to groom a horse well, but they were definitely getting a lesson from the man Nigel introduced as Mark. Majesty, Nigel's horse, didn't just look good. He looked perfect! And then Mark worked some more.

"This isn't an event where the grooming matters much to the judges," Nigel explained. "But the audience expects the horses to look good, and careful grooming matters to the horses as well. They simply perform better when they know they look good. Horses can be quite vain, you know."

"I've always thought it was just that they liked all the attention they get with a careful grooming," Carole said.

"Definitely part of it," Nigel agreed. "Whatever it is, it works."

"Well, whatever Mark does, it works," Stevie said, still impressed with the results of the groom's ministrations. "I think we could get some pointers here."

"You probably could, but I'm going to shoo you back to your seats. The show is starting in a few minutes, and though I'd be glad to have you stay around, the show management discourages visitors during the performance. My event is the last of the evening, so I won't be seeing you again tonight, but I gather you'll be at the stable when Doro and I get there tomorrow."

Doro? Stevie thought. Then she realized that, of course, he was talking about Dorothy. She liked the nickname. She smiled.

"Yes, tomorrow. We'll be there. Promise," she said.

They all shook his hand and listened carefully while he gave them directions to get back to their seats. They made only three or four wrong turns (depending on whether it was Stevie's count or Lisa's), but they made it, and by the time the horn sounded to announce the beginning of the first event, they were back in their seats next to Max and Mrs. Reg.

"Did you meet Nigel?" Max asked Lisa, who sat next to him.

Lisa nodded. "He's wonderful," she said. "Just right for Dorothy."

"I think so, too," Max said.

The show began.

10

ALTHOUGH THERE WASN'T anything about horses that the girls didn't like, there were things they liked better than others, and there was one thing they were definitely looking forward to. The classes before the Gambler's Choice couldn't hold a candle to it in excitement. Besides that, they didn't know any of the riders in the other classes, and they knew one in the Gambler's Choice—three if they counted the two team members that Nigel had introduced them to.

When it was almost time for Nigel's class, the ring was cleared and swept, and then the roustabouts took a long time setting up the jumps.

"They have to be just so," Carole explained to her

friends, though they already knew something about setting up jumps for a competition. "The woman there with the clipboard is probably the course designer. It's a very specialized career. . . ."

Stevie loved Carole a lot, but she did sometimes wish that her friend wouldn't go on and on. When the subject was horses, there was almost no way to stop her once she began. Stevie tried, though.

"Is that one of the careers you've considered?" Stevie asked.

Carole paused and looked at Stevie. The twinkle in her eye told Carole she was teasing.

"I was doing it again, huh?"

"Yes, you were. Fortunately, I was here to stop you, and now the event is going to begin, which will stop me from gloating!"

It was times like that that made both Carole and Stevie glad they were best friends. They shook hands. Lisa joined in.

The first part of the event was allowing all the riders to walk the course. All the competitors, about twenty-five of them, came out at once. Unlike most jump courses, this one didn't have a specified order that the riders had to follow. Instead, each jump had a point value, and they could choose whatever jumps they wanted. They could go over any jumps, up to two times, during the first fifty seconds of the competition. Then, when the final buzzer rang, they had fifteen seconds in which to decide whether or not they would jump The Joker. That was the highest, toughest jump of all. If they missed, they lost. If they made it, they got seventy points. If they didn't attempt it, they weren't penalized, but they also wouldn't be likely to win.

"Look, there's Nigel!" Lisa said, pointing him out to her friends. It wasn't really necessary, though, because he'd already spotted them and was walking over to measure the part of the course that ran right by them.

"I'm riding seventeenth," he told them.

"Oh, that's great!" said Max. It was considered an advantage to be riding late because then the rider would know what score he or she had to beat.

Just as the ring was being cleared, Dorothy joined them in their seats. Max told her that Nigel was riding seventeenth, but she already knew that.

"And he's the first member of his team, too. They all drew high numbers."

Although Nigel and his teammates were at the show as a team, this was an individual event, not a team event, and each rider was entered on his or her own behalf. However, teammates were always happy when a friend did well.

The event began.

It took a few of the riders going through the course for the Saddle Club girls to get used to the way it was done. They'd seen plenty of jumping before, but never this daring and never this fast.

"And never this *good*," Stevie added to Carole's thoughts.

The riders were pressed for time, trying to make as many high-valued jumps as possible in the first fifty seconds. Max had spent a lot of time teaching his riders how important form was in jumping, but in this event, form went out the window. The only thing that counted was getting over the jump, high and fast.

In the jumping that Max taught them, it was important to keep the horse at a steady gait. Steadiness was much more important than speed. That was not the case here. Also, in the jumping they usually did, if the horse knocked the top of the fence, there would be penalty deductions. In this event, the only consequence of a "tick" was that the audience would *ooooooh* and *aaaaaah* until they knew whether the bar would fall down or not. The audience seemed to like the suspense and clapped every time the bar was hit.

The horses had a lot of trouble with the forty-point

jump, and it wasn't surprising, since it was the most valuable jump next to The Joker, and everybody wanted to try it. There was no penalty for a knockdown; it was just that no points accumulated and precious time was lost.

Most of the riders concentrated on the twenty-five- and thirty-point jumps. Anything less than that wasn't worth trying, except that there was a ten-pointer on the way to the thirty-point jump, and almost everybody went over it.

Each time the buzzer announced the end of the first fifty seconds, there was a breathless silence in the arena. Would the rider try The Joker? It loomed far higher than any of the other jumps. It was over six feet tall. Because the riders didn't stand a chance if they didn't try it, most did. There were a few exceptions. One rider who was having trouble controlling his horse decided to pass on it. Since he'd accumulated only forty-five points in the first fifty seconds, there was no way he was in contention to win anyway.

Another rider decided to play it very safe. Her horse had done extremely well on the regular jumps, and she'd accumulated enough points there that perhaps she thought she had a shot at a prize without gambling, so she passed on it.

Among those who did try it, not many made it. By Carole's count, it was just a little over half. But it was clear from just watching that those who did were the best of the best. Any rider who competed in this show was good. The ones who did well were excellent. It was a real treat for the girls, and they enjoyed every second of it.

They particularly enjoyed the seventy-five seconds in which Nigel was riding the course.

Dorothy sat forward in her seat, and Lisa could have sworn she didn't breathe the entire time Nigel was riding. He chose a daring course for himself, attempting the hardest jumps and ignoring the easy ten-point fences.

Nigel's horse was as wonderful in motion as he had been standing still. But Stevie admired his grooming even more when the horse was cantering and jumping. The horse seemed to fly over the jumps, rising effortlessly in the air, almost hovering at the apex of the jump and then landing smoothly.

"Oh," Lisa said. It was so beautiful, it took her breath away.

Then the buzzer sounded, and Nigel had to make up his mind about The Joker. He didn't really have to make up his mind, Carole realized. His mind had been made up a long time ago. He was going to go for it.

He circled his horse around, curving smoothly past the edge of the jump, too close, really, for the horse to get a good look and become frightened. And then, at the last minute, Nigel had the horse turn, and before the horse knew what was happening, they were headed straight for it.

Nigel rose in his saddle, putting all his weight on his stirrups, yet keeping his legs perfectly still. He leaned forward, moved his hands forward, and signaled his horse that it was time.

The horse didn't have to be told twice. He rose as smoothly to jump this huge fence as he had to go over the little ones. His feet pawed ever so slightly at the air above the fence and then stretched forward, reaching for the ground, where he landed with a soft *pfffft*.

Dorothy stood up and applauded for Nigel. So did Max and Mrs. Reg. Stevie and her friends joined them. Stevie even let out a polite "Yaaaaay."

Nigel had scored well. It was too early to see how the other riders would do, but he was certainly in contention for a ribbon and a cash prize. Dorothy thought that was great.

There were two more riders, then, neither of whom did very well. One missed The Joker. The next didn't even attempt it since her horse hadn't been able to succeed even on the forty-point fence. Then came Camilla Wentworth on Elementary.

The girls looked at the horse carefully and still could see no sign of anything wrong with him. His ears flicked alertly, and his eyes shot around the arena curiously. He pranced, rather than walked, into the arena while the public-address system introduced him and his rider.

Camilla seemed a little perturbed. Elementary wasn't being any more difficult than many of the other horses had been, but Carole and her friends knew from experience that a horse who wasn't behaving the way that horse usually behaved could be trouble. Carole hoped that wasn't the case here.

Elementary took off like a shot when Camilla was ready to go over the first jump. He flew over that jump and the one that followed. But there was something wrong. Even if most of the audience didn't know it, anyone who could see Camilla's face knew it. Elementary was giving her trouble, a lot of it.

Camilla wanted him to go over the forty-point jump, but he seemed bound and determined to go over the thirty. She had to flick him with her riding crop to get him to go where she wanted him to go. This was definitely bad news. It wasn't that the riding crop hurt him. It was merely an aid to getting him to do what he was supposed to do. The problem was that he shouldn't have needed it. In a competition situation, a seasoned horse should respond better.

Figuring that going over the thirty-point jump was better than refusal from Elementary, Camilla allowed him to go over it and then tried to take him back over the forty-pointer. He was having none of it. She rode directly at the jump, rose in the saddle, and signaled him to jump. Instead, he stopped dead in his tracks.

Ooooooooh, the audience said.

Camilla turned the horse around and retreated about fifteen feet, enough space to allow him to get to his takeoff speed, and tried again. This time, instead of just stopping, Elementary bucked and then reared. He yanked his head to one side.

Camilla did everything she could to stay on the horse, and in the end she managed to do that, but the violent yanking of the horse's head pulled very hard at her left arm. Her right hand kept holding the reins firmly, but the left one released them completely. To the dismay of the audience, Camilla's left arm simply dropped limply to her side.

Everyone in the arena stood up to see what was happening and to lend support to a rider in trouble. Unfortunately, it wasn't going to change the fact that Camilla was hurt and couldn't complete the course.

While the audience applauded politely, Camilla rode Elementary out of the ring.

"She was having a problem before with her horse," Carole said to Dorothy. "She even asked Nigel to look at it. They couldn't find anything wrong with him."

"Maybe he's just in a bad mood," Dorothy said. "That happens. Every horse has good days and bad days. This is clearly a bad one for Elementary."

"Is she going to be okay?" Stevie asked.

"Oh, sure," Dorothy said. "Looks like she dislocated her arm. She'll be better soon. It hurts like crazy, especially when they get a couple of strong guys to hold you and put the joint back where it belongs, but she'll be as good as new and back in the saddle in a couple of weeks or a . . ."

Dorothy's voice trailed off.

"Oh, no! I've got to see Nigel!" she said. Without another word, she stood up and left the seats.

The Pine Hollow riders looked at one another.

"I guess that's what it's like when you're engaged," Stevie said philosophically. "When you've got to see the man you love, there's just no stopping you."

The girls smiled. It did seem so romantic—if a little bit odd.

A few minutes later, the public-address system announced that Camilla Wentworth had, in fact, dislocated her shoulder and been taken to the hospital, where she was expected to recover completely. That sounded like good news.

When the last of the competitors had finished the course, it turned out that Nigel had taken third place. That meant that he'd won a nice prize that would no doubt help to pay for the couple's honeymoon.

The Saddle Club was disappointed that they didn't get to see Nigel and Dorothy again, but it was late, there was a lot of work to do for tomorrow, and Max was ready to take them all back to Stevie's.

"You'll see Dorothy and Nigel tomorrow," Max reminded them.

That also reminded them about their wonderful surprise for Max. It was going to be quite an April Fools' Day!

11

THREE VERY SLEEPY riders arrived at Pine Hollow the following morning at six-thirty. Stevie had kept the girls up until very late the night (morning!) before, and it had been quite a struggle to get out of bed in the morning. Lisa wasn't sure she could remember having gone to bed at all. Carole could remember it. She remembered it so well that she wasn't sure she'd actually ever gotten up!

They each carried a bag of flowers, which they took into the tack room where they were going to work. They'd finished making crowns for the bridal party and a bouquet for the "bride's" rider. All they had left to do was to make the grape arbor into a bower. Stevie called it the "bridal path," and the girls liked the pun. It was one of the few things that they liked that early in the morning.

"Come on, let's get this stuff inside. Max and Mrs. Reg won't be here for another half an hour, so we've got time to assemble the floral bower. Then they'll be too busy with the weekend riders to notice what we're up to until Horse Wise starts at ten, right?"

"Of course you're right," Lisa said drowsily. It seemed easier than trying to think about how anything might go wrong.

They worked in rare silence for half an hour, chaining the flowers together. Then, as each chain got long enough, two of the girls carried it out to the arbor and put it across the top. Tired as they all were, the girls had to admit that it looked fabulous. It was hard to keep from smiling when something was going to look so pretty—especially when it was finished. There was still plenty of work to do.

The tack room was around the corner from Mrs. Reg's office—out of her sight, but close enough so that the girls would know when Mrs. Reg got there. That was an important thing to know, because Mrs. Reg was amazing in several respects, one of which was that she always knew everything that was going on in her stable. No matter how secretive the girls tried to be, if they were still weaving flowers when Mrs. Reg arrived, they were convinced that she'd know it.

An hour and a half seemed like enough time, but an hour definitely was not. When Mrs. Reg broke her pattern and arrived at 7:30, the girls were upset. The whole tack room was still filled with flowers, and the grape arbor wasn't! They hoped against hope that Mrs. Reg wouldn't make her usual morning rounds to check everything, and they worked as quietly as mice.

Stevie cracked open the door to the tack room so they could hear when Mrs. Reg might be coming their way. Instead, they got quite a surprise. The person with her was Dorothy DeSoto.

"Probably here to sign the papers to sell Geronimo," Carole whispered. That seemed logical, but it didn't explain the fact that there was a distinct sound of crying coming from Mrs. Reg's office. Was Dorothy *that* fond of Geronimo? She'd be able to come and visit him anytime. This didn't make sense.

The girls strained to listen. The words were muffled and the message was unclear. They heard things like: "Nothing's working . . . Mother . . . disappointed . . . all the guests . . . all the *presents* . . . I can't believe it . . . six whole weeks!" The girls didn't like the sound of this at all. They leaned toward the door of the tack room so they could hear better.

Pretty soon they dropped all pretense of working with their flowers and moved toward the tack-room door to hear better. That wasn't quite good enough. They opened the door wider.

". . . cancel the caterer . . . minister going on vacation . . . love him so!"

They stepped out into the hall.

". . . honeymoon . . . Acapulco . . . Oh, Mrs. Reg, I just can't stand it!"

That was enough. The girls just had to know. Without a word among them, they walked into Mrs. Reg's office.

There was Dorothy DeSoto and a whole box of tissues, most of which seemed to have been used and scattered on the floor. Her face was red from crying. It occurred to Lisa that they might be interrupting something rather private, but such thoughts rarely crossed Stevie's mind. She barged right in.

"What happened?" she asked.

"It's Camilla," Dorothy began, but then she was overwhelmed with tears.

"I thought she was going to be all right," said Lisa. "It's just a dislocated shoulder, isn't it?"

"Did something happen to Elementary?" Carole

asked. It would certainly occur to Carole first that the problem might be equine, rather than human.

Dorothy took a deep breath, wiped away two more tears, and tried to explain the situation. "No, they're both okay. I mean, sort of. Yes, Camilla dislocated her shoulder and she'll be fine—in *six* weeks. And Elementary is just fine. This morning he was his usual calm, steady, professional self, so we'll never know what was going on in his mind last night."

Just the act of having to explain seemed to have set Dorothy on the road to recovery. She sniffed and wiped as she spoke, but at least she was talking.

"The problem is that Camilla won't be able to ride for six weeks, and the team is competing in some very important shows during those particular six weeks, and they just can't be a person short. That means that they have to use the alternates, but there are only two qualified alternates at this time, and one of them is eight months pregnant, so she can't ride at all."

"So, what about the other one?" Lisa asked.

"The other one was to replace Nigel while we"— here the tears started tumbling again, but Dorothy continued in spite of them—"got married and went on our honeymoon!" The final word overwhelmed her.

"I think I get the picture here," Lisa said, sorting it out for her friends. "Because Camilla can't ride, Nigel *has* to. He could probably beg off, but that would be unprofessional, and Nigel is very professional."

Dorothy nodded vigorously.

"So the problem is that Dorothy's wedding is scheduled to take place on Long Island next weekend, and it will be missing only one thing: the groom!"

The tears continued.

"Why can't you get married before that?" Carole asked.

Dorothy blew her nose, tossed another tissue onto the floor, and answered the question. "We can, of course, but it was going to be such a beautiful wedding. It wasn't going to be big, but it was going to be at my stables, and it was going to be nice. I think that's what bothers me the most. We can reschedule our honeymoon. Camilla promises she'll be better in six weeks, and even if she isn't, the team can be one person short after these next few important shows. So we won't have a problem then."

"It's the wedding part," Stevie said very sympathetically. "I know how it is. A girl dreams about her wedding for years. She plans it from earliest girlhood —the most important day of her life—and you can't stand the idea that all your dreams of a perfect wedding have been dashed against the rocks of misfortune."

Carole and Lisa looked at Stevie. When she started talking about things like dreams being dashed against the rocks of misfortune, she was up to something. Carole looked down at the flowers she still held in her hand, and she knew what it was that Stevie was thinking.

"Some girls want to have big church weddings with thousands of guests. Others like the idea of a small chapel, maybe outdoors, with a few close friends. Others, like you, want to be surrounded by the people and the creatures you love best. . . ."

Dorothy nodded. "Yes, I really wanted to get married at my stable."

"How about Max's instead?" Stevie asked.

"Here?"

"And now," Stevie said.

"Now?"

Stevie looked at her watch and shrugged. "Well, maybe around ten o'clock when the chairs will be set up and the hors d'oeuvres will have arrived. You do like apple slices and sugar lumps, don't you?"

"What are you talking about?" Mrs. Reg asked.

"Can't you tell? We're planning a wedding," Lisa answered for Stevie.

111

"For whom?" Mrs. Reg asked.

It was such a totally logical question to a totally illogical situation that the girls could only laugh. It took a minute to explain.

"Wait a minute!" Mrs. Reg said. "I remember now. I even had a mark on my calendar. This is April Fools' Day, isn't it? Look what I wrote."

She held the calendar out. Right there on April 1, in Mrs. Reg's neat handwriting, it said, "Keep an eye on Stevie!"

That was enough to get Dorothy to stop crying. First, she picked up all of her tissues, then she stood up to hug the girls.

"You three are something else—really something else. I can't tell you how much you've cheered me up with your wonderful, but practically impossible, idea. I know Nigel and I will get married one day, it's just that circumstances have . . ." Her lip quivered.

"Well, we have the whole thing planned. We thought Geronimo ought to have a proper welcome, and a wedding seemed like a good idea," Carole explained, trying to refocus Dorothy on happy thoughts instead of sad ones. Mrs. Reg was almost out of tissues anyway. "It seemed nice and romantic!"

"And it would be," Dorothy agreed. "Nigel and I will be here for it. I guess we'll be the only ones on the groom's side of the chapel, though?" Dorothy clearly didn't realize yet that the girls were serious. Stevie's mind was racing. Her thoughts were interrupted by a new arrival.

"What's going on in here?" said a newly familiar, very British voice. "I thought there would be nothing but tears. We have laughter!"

"Oh, Nigel, you'll never guess what these girls have been up to!"

"A miracle cure for a dislocated shoulder?" he asked hopefully.

"Almost as good," Dorothy said, and then she shared the secret of the April Fools' Horse Wise meeting.

Nigel smiled as he listened. Once again Lisa was struck by what a warm and wonderful smile he had.

"Doro warned me about you three," he teased. "Is there nothing you can't accomplish?"

They looked around at one another. Stevie shrugged. "Nothing so far," she said.

"Well, I don't suppose you could come up with a minister for us, could you?"

Naturally, Stevie's mind clicked into gear. She didn't think it would be too good of an idea for her to call the minister at her family's church. He hadn't been very enthusiastic about some of her pranks the last time she'd been allowed to go to Sunday school. He apparently didn't share her sense of humor.

"I don't think so," she said. "That's the one thing we can't do for you. We do have a photographer, some horses to ride, a bridal bouquet—even a garter, though it's the right size for Delilah, and I don't know how Dorothy's legs compare to hers. . . ."

"Very well, I daresay," Nigel joked. Then he patted his pocket. "You know, I just picked up our rings from the jeweler. Do you think they would fit the horses?" Everybody but Stevie laughed. She was still thinking.

Dorothy took Nigel's hand and stood up. She turned to the girls. "You're simply wonderful to have come up with this terrific scheme. I know Max is going to enjoy it. A little romance never hurt anyone— even Geronimo. And I love the idea that we can be there, even if we're not in starring roles. So count us in. In the meantime, however, this stable has a new stallion, and he's in the van out front. Is there anyone who could leave flower weaving long enough to help us put Geronimo in his paddock, where he can get a really good view of his wedding?"

The three girls volunteered. First they put their un-

114

woven flowers back into the tack room, and then they went out front where the van from Dorothy's stable was parked.

Geronimo was quite a handful. Dorothy wouldn't let the girls hold his lead, but she did let them help her with the van and the ramp, and while she and Nigel led Geronimo to his paddock, the girls put away the ramp and began to close up the van.

A car pulled up behind the van and honked because the van was blocking its way. Stevie and Lisa finished stowing the ramp while Carole went to explain to the driver what was going on.

Carole was dismayed to see that the driver was cranky old Judge Gavin, but he smiled when he saw her.

"We're just finishing with the unloading, Your Honor," she said. "It'll only be a minute."

"No problem," he said. "I'm a little early anyway. And I'm glad to see you, Carole. I was looking for you last week because I don't know how to thank you for suggesting that I ride that mare."

There was something about the way Judge Gavin said that that made the wheels begin to turn in Carole's head in a very Stevie-like way. She cleared her throat.

115

"Actually, Your Honor, I've just thought of a way you might be able to thank me. Could I ask you a tiny little favor?"

"Ask away," he said.

She did.

12

STEVIE GAVE A little wave. Just as planned, May Grover pushed the button. There was a brief delay, and then the music started.

Here comes the bride . . .

Stevie hummed and sang to herself. It was wonderful! It was perfect!

Then she gave Topside a little nudge, and he began walking. She adjusted her shiny top hat, setting it at a jaunty angle, and then ducked as Topside entered the grape arbor.

The wedding was beginning.

Lisa rode right next to her and Carole followed them, on Starlight. At the first note of the music, everybody in the audience stood up, mostly because Mrs. Reg told them to. Stevie could hear her whispering to the kids. But as the processional began, even the reluctant Pony Club members were all standing. Nobody wanted to miss anything.

Stevie, Carole, and Lisa rode slowly and in a dignified manner. Stevie felt as if she were in a parade. She smiled at the people who were watching. They smiled back. Some even waved. She didn't wave back. That wouldn't be dignified.

When they reached the front of the makeshift chapel, Stevie, Carole, and Lisa drew their horses to the side. Nigel was there, riding Comanche. Max, the last-minute best man, was next to Nigel. And there, in front of all of them and facing all of them, was none other than Judge Gavin, riding Delilah.

Carole smiled to herself as she watched him. He'd agreed to her favor immediately, as long as he could do it riding Delilah, and as long as he could have some pictures from the wedding. In fact, he'd thought pictures were such a good idea that he'd called the local newspaper, who'd sent a reporter and a photographer immediately. Carole was sure Judge Gavin's enthusiasm stemmed from his devotion to romance, and his commitment to family values, but she suspected it also had something to do with a tough re-election campaign that he had coming up in the fall.

Nearby stood Geronimo. He'd come over to the corner of his new paddock nearest to the festivities. It seemed very right that he be involved. It seemed even more right that Delilah was right up at the front where all the action was!

"Oooooooh!" That's what the young riders said when Dorothy emerged from the grape arbor. It had taken a good deal of time and effort and all of Stevie's skills, but there was no question who the bride was at this wedding.

Dorothy was wearing a pearl-gray sidesaddle riding habit. There hadn't been anything in white. She was riding Pepper, whose gray coat seemed to go perfectly with her outfit. It looked as if she'd stepped straight out of the nineteenth century, too. She had a white silk blouse with a white stock held in place by Mrs. Reg's horse pin with a diamond eye that sparkled in the early April sunshine. Her veil had been a real challenge. The outfit had a hat, but it was a riding hat, not the kind of thing you wanted to get married in. There had been a long discussion of just how to handle it. In the end, Stevie had prevailed. The mosquito netting was draped dramatically over her head and then held in place with a crown of fresh flowers, pinned to her hairdo.

"I don't think you can do better for a zillion dollars," Stevie had declared looking at the finished product. Dorothy looked simply beautiful.

It did occur to Lisa that it wasn't good practice to be on a horse without a hard hat, but she felt that Dorothy's wedding ought to be a rare exception to that, so she didn't even raise the issue.

Dorothy drew to a halt in front of Judge Gavin. Nigel moved over toward her so that they stood side by side.

"Dearly beloved," Judge Gavin began.

Ten minutes later, Nigel leaned over in his saddle and kissed Dorothy. They were married!

With that Dorothy tossed her bouquet up in the air. Much to Judge Gavin's surprise, it landed in *his* lap, startling him and Delilah.

Stevie, Lisa, and Carole all looked at one another. As far as they were concerned, it wasn't Judge Gavin who'd caught the bouquet at all. It was Delilah, and that was as it should be. After all, she *was* going to be the next one married!

The bridesmaids couldn't help themselves. They turned to one another and gave each other high fives.

Then the newlyweds turned their horses around and walked back out of the chapel. Stevie didn't even have to give May a signal this time. She knew she was supposed to push the button on the tape deck, and she did. Then, instead of traditional rice, the members of the wedding party began tossing handfuls of oats at Nigel and Dorothy.

"Only you would think of something like this, Stevie! Only you!" Dorothy said. And then, because it was so true, everybody laughed and then clapped while Dorothy and Nigel rode out under the grape arbor.

They didn't ride far, though. There was still a party to be had. Stevie, Lisa, and Carole took their horses, as well as Nigel's and Dorothy's, and put them in their stalls, giving them each a quick grooming and a promise of more to come. Carole offered to stable Delilah, but Judge Gavin said he hadn't really had his weekly ride yet, so he thought he would pass on the reception and go straight into the woods.

Once again Carole thanked him. He said it had been his pleasure and he really did want a couple of copies of the photographs that the official wedding photographer, Adam Levine, had taken, rather than just the ones the newspaper had snapped. Carole promised to send him a set. Then she gave Delilah a pat and a hug and wished the judge a very happy trail ride. She also slipped Delilah a piece of carrot and a sugar lump. It seemed to her to be the very least she could do for the "other" bride at the wedding.

Then the party began in earnest. It turned out that when Pony Clubbers put their minds to it, they could assemble a very nice party. They were all delighted that Max's surprise birthday party turned out to be a horse wedding that turned out to be a people wedding. When Stevie and her friends were involved, switches like that were simply to be expected. A couple of the girls said that they might have dressed up more if they'd known what was going to happen. Two others confessed to Stevie that this was exactly the wedding they'd always dreamed of for themselves.

Stevie was a little surprised at that. She thought she was the only one who had weird dreams!

"Apple? Sugar lump?" she said, offering a tray of hors d'oeuvres to Max.

"Uh, sure," he said, taking a slice of apple and leaving the sugar lump behind. He also took a glass of ginger ale. "Say, tell me something, Stevie."

"Anything, Max," she said.

"What was going on here? I mean, I have the distinct impression that I just served as the best man at the wedding of two people who actually got married, but I haven't got the faintest idea of how it happened. The last thing I knew, my mother was telling me to mount up and smile."

"You did a very good job of it, too," Stevie said. "You didn't even lose the ring."

"Here, Max, try some of these carrot sticks," Carole said, offering him the bowl.

He took one absentmindedly and bit into it. "Nice," he said. "But then, everything here is. I mean, look at all these flowers! When did you do all this? How long have you known that Camilla Wentworth was going to dislocate her shoulder?"

"We didn't," Stevie said. "It was just that it seemed like a good idea to plan a wedding for today, and we figured a bride and groom would come along, somehow."

Max regarded her carefully.

"You know," he said, "from anybody else, I would know that they were joking, but from you, I'm not so sure."

Stevie smiled beatifically.

"I think that means I should just enjoy myself at the party, right?"

"Right," Stevie said. "Everybody else is. Why shouldn't you?"

With that, Max headed for the drink table to pour

himself another glass of ginger ale in a champagne glass.

The whole wedding was so perfect and so much fun that even snobby Veronica diAngelo couldn't find anything to complain about, except the fact that the cake she'd brought wasn't getting enough attention. That all changed, however, when Stevie unveiled it in its new and improved format.

She had brought a few of her own model horses to put on top of the cake as the bride and groom, but when it turned out that there were actually going to be people getting married, that wasn't going to be good enough. She'd gone to May, who happened to have her Ken and Barbie dolls in her backpack. Ken and Barbie were dressed for a camping trip, not a wedding, but they were definitely better than nothing. Stevie seated one on each of the two model horses and, miraculously, it was a perfect wedding cake!

"Have you forgotten anything?" Mrs. Reg asked, amazed at the total party that her young riders had managed to create without her knowing anything about it.

Nigel and Dorothy came over to cut the cake. Dorothy removed one of the model horses from the top of it and even had the good sense to lick the frosting from the horses' hooves. Nigel picked up the other and followed suit.

"Very good!" he said. "Who did this? Can I have the recipe?"

"I did," Veronica said, raising her hand. Then noticing a scowl from Stevie, she corrected herself. "Actually our *cook* made it. I'll have her send Dorothy the recipe."

"No," Dorothy said. "Have her send it to Nigel. He's a much better cook than I am."

"But you're better at microwaving than I am," he teased her.

"Look! Their very first fight!" Stevie exclaimed.

Then everybody laughed.

Before too long, it was time for Dorothy and Nigel to leave. They had to get him to the airport for a six o'clock flight to Italy, and Dorothy had to drive back to Long Island to take care of her horses and explain to her mother why she wasn't getting married next Saturday.

All the members of Horse Wise pitched in to help with the cleanup, but it didn't turn out to be much work. Most of the food had been eaten, and with Max's approval, they decided to leave the flowers on the grape arbor for a day or so until they wilted. There were chairs to be folded, paper cups to be thrown away, and soda bottles to be recycled. The party goers had been neat, so there wasn't a lot of garbage.

By the time the last paper cup had been routed out from where it was wedged under the fence, Adam Levine showed up with the pictures from the wedding. He'd taken them to a one-hour photo place, and they were all ready!

"Look! There are the bridesmaids!"

"You look so great!"

"Not as great as the bride!"

"Oh, Adam, you got a picture of Comanche trying to nip at Delilah!" That had been a tense moment in the wedding. Fortunately, Nigel was such a good rider that he'd controlled the horse perfectly. Judge Gavin wouldn't have known what to do if Delilah had gotten into a battle!

"And look! There they are, kissing!"

They were. It was a sweet photograph of Dorothy and Nigel, taken while the two of them were on horseback, newly wed and kissing.

"But what's Delilah looking at there?" somebody asked. "While all this kissing is going on, she seems to be staring off into the distance. I wonder what she sees."

Carole looked at the picture and then showed it to Lisa and Stevie. There wasn't any question what

Delilah was looking at. Her eyes were glued to Geronimo.

"Ooooooh, I love weddings!" one of the young riders cooed.

Stevie, Lisa, and Carole couldn't have agreed more. They just weren't sure that anybody else knew exactly who—or what—had gotten married that day!

THE THREE GIRLS were sprawled around Carole's living room later that day, too tired to do anything but talk. Stevie had claimed Colonel Hanson's recliner. Carole lay on the sofa, and Lisa had taken some pillows to make herself a soft spot on the floor. What they were waiting for was eight P.M., when Skye Ransom's television wedding was due to take place. They had some time before then. They had things to say to one another.

"We're terrific, you know," Stevie said modestly.

"Yeah," Lisa agreed.

"Right," said Carole. "We can accomplish anything. I mean, we did weeks and weeks worth of organizing work for Max just this last week, and that gave Max enough time to get us tickets to go to the horse show, which was absolutely wonderful. . . ."

"What did you say?" Colonel Hanson asked, walking into the living room with a very large bowl of popcorn, some glasses, and some soda. The girls abandoned their comfortable spots to be near the popcorn bowl. That allowed the colonel to reclaim his recliner.

"I said we did a lot of work for Max this week so he would have time to get us the tickets to the show."

"Hmmm. Very interesting."

"What's interesting, Dad?" Carole asked.

"It's interesting that he called me a week ago and said he had the tickets, and would it be all right for you to go with him. He also said he was calling Stevie's and Lisa's parents."

"You mean a week ago like last Saturday?"

"Just like last Saturday," the colonel confirmed. "In fact, he said that Dorothy and Nigel had gotten him five perfectly wonderful seats, and he felt you three deserved a treat. He didn't tell you that?"

"He did *not*," Carole said.

"Definitely did not," Lisa added.

"Grrrrrrr," was all Stevie could say.

"We would have done the work anyway," Carole

said. "Remember all the work we did when Mrs. Reg went away? We always like to pitch in."

"He didn't have to trick us. He never has to trick us."

"Grrrrrrr."

Colonel Hanson abandoned his recliner and left the girls to their musings.

"We like doing things for Max," Carole reasoned. "We always say yes when he asks."

"We would have done just as good a job," said Lisa.

"Grrrrrr."

Then Stevie's face brightened. "I've got it," she said. "It was his April Fools' joke on us."

"Why would he do that? He's never played a trick on us before," said Lisa. "Has he?"

"No, but we've played lots on him. Maybe that was just turnabout. That's fair, isn't it?"

Carole wasn't so certain. "Now, let me get this straight," she said. "For years you've been playing April Fools' jokes on Max and getting away with it. Then this year he decides on revenge, only instead of just playing a trick on you, we worked like crazy all week because he was playing a trick on all three of us?"

"Something like that," Stevie said. "It has to be."

130

"That's not fair! We didn't play any tricks on him at all!" Lisa said.

"Well, not quite," said Stevie.

Lisa and Carole didn't like the sound of that and asked her what it meant.

"It meant I couldn't resist," said Stevie.

"Doing what?" Lisa asked.

"Well, remember when you guys were in the tack room packing your bags and folding all our wedding clothes?"

"Where were you?" Carole asked.

"I was in the stable," said Stevie. "I had to do some moving. I had to move all the horses. I moved every one of them over one stall to the left. The one on the far left end, I moved to the far right end."

"You what?"

"I moved every one of them over one stall to the—"

"We heard you," Lisa said. "But why did you do that?"

"I sort of couldn't resist," Stevie said. "You know how it is when the urge comes over me?"

They did know, and they weren't always sure they liked it, but this time, they might make an exception.

"How's Max going to know who did it?"

"Who else would do something like that?" Carole asked.

"Maybe," said Stevie. "But I didn't want to leave it to chance. So I did a little something with the hat wall."

"Yes?"

"I moved the hats around so that they spell 'April Fool!' "

"That'll do it," Lisa said. "Max will definitely figure it out."

"And I'm glad I did."

"I am, too," said Lisa. "I didn't mind doing all that work, really. In fact, some of it, like the clothes part, was really fun. But it was a little sneaky to trick us into doing the work."

"You're right," said Carole. "He deserved it. Nice going, Stevie."

Then she checked the clock. It was just three minutes until eight. The girls poured themselves sodas, retreated to their chosen soft seats, and Carole clicked on the television so they could watch their second wedding of the day.

"Third, if we count Dorothy and Nigel's!" Stevie said. They all laughed.

Skye's wedding was really nice, but the girls agreed that it could have used a few special touches.

132

"Like some horses," Lisa said.

The phone rang then. Carole stood up and went into the kitchen to answer it. Lisa and Stevie stayed in the living room, picking up little pieces of popcorn and wiping off the tables so everything would be clean.

A few minutes later, Carole returned to the living room.

"It was your mother, Stevie," she said.

Stevie stood up to get the phone.

"No, she's off the phone now," Carole explained. "She just called to say that your room was a mess and you will have to have it cleaned up right away or you won't go riding on Tuesday. She sounded really angry."

"Oh, no," Stevie said, recalling the disaster area she sometimes called her room. She'd meant to clean it up. She really had. But The Saddle Club had been so busy with the wedding and the horse show the night before. Her mother would understand. She just *had* to. There was no way she could get it *all* done by Tuesday, but maybe if she got a good start on it—or if she got some help?

"You wouldn't mind giving me a hand, would you?" Stevie asked.

"No way," said Lisa.

"Uh-uh," said Carole.

"Please?"

"Nope."

"I'm going to miss class then for sure!"

"Too bad," said Lisa. "You're going to have to do it yourself this time, though."

"Aw, come on. It won't take us long."

"Us?"

Stevie seemed truly despondent. Carole thought it had gone on long enough. After all, the phone call was simply somebody selling magazine subscriptions.

Carole grinned at Stevie. "April Fool!" she announced.

"Really?"

"Really," Carole said.

"You had me going!" Stevie said. "I thought it really was my mother. How did you figure that trick out?"

"I've learned from a pro," Carole said.

"Thanks," Stevie said, accepting that as a compliment. For all the members, there was something just wonderful about being in The Saddle Club, and it had to do with being appreciated for what they were. They were friends.

ABOUT THE AUTHOR

BONNIE BRYANT is the author of more than fifty books for young readers, including novelizations of movie hits such as *Teenage Mutant Ninja Turtles* and *Honey, I Blew Up the Kid*, written under her married name, B. B. Hiller.

Ms. Bryant began writing The Saddle Club in 1986. Although she had done some riding before that, she intensified her studies then and found herself learning right along with her characters Stevie, Carole, and Lisa. She claims that they are all much better riders than she is.

Ms. Bryant was born and raised in New York City. She lives in Greenwich Village with her two sons.

T·H·E
SADDLE CLUB

A blue-ribbon series by Bonnie Bryant

Stevie, Carole and Lisa are all very different, but they *love* horses!
The three girls are best friends at Pine Hollow Stables, where they
ride and care for all kinds of horses. Come to Pine Hollow and get
ready for all the fun and adventure that comes with being 13!

**Watch for other THE SADDLE CLUB books all year.
More great reading—and riding to come!**